DIE LETHAL

Adam Millard is the author of twenty-seven novels, seventeen novellas, and more than two hundred short stories, which can be found in various collections and anthologies. Probably best known for his post-apocalyptic fiction, Adam also writes fantasy/horror for children, as well as bizarro fiction for several publishers. His work has been translated for the German, Spanish, and Russian markets. He lives in Newcastle-under-Lyme with his wife, Dawn, and his two cats, Butter and Toast.

Copyright 2024 Adam Millard
This Edition Published 2024 by Crowded Quarantine Publications
The moral right of the author has been asserted
All characters in this publication are fictitious and any resemblance to real persons, living or dead, is purely coincidental.

All rights reserved.
No part of this publication may be reproduced, stored in a retrieval system, or transmitted, in any form or by any means without the prior permission in writing of the publisher, nor be otherwise circulated in any form of binding or cover other than that in which it is published and without a similar condition including this condition being imposed on the subsequent purchase.
A CIP catalogue record for this book is available from the British Library

ISBN: 978-1-7384764-8-0

Crowded Quarantine Publications
124 Dimsdale Parade West
Newcastle-Under-Lyme. Staffordshire
ST5 8DU

DIE LETHAL

ADAM MILLARD

1

It was a beautiful day in LA. People were going about their business as usual, which is to say that a lot of them were standing on corners, arguing with one another about what the best pizzeria over on Westside was, now that *Mission: Impizzable* had burnt to the ground. Word on the street was: *The DaVinci Crust* used far too much sauce and *Mama's Pizzeria and Crematorium (Your Loss is Our Sauce!) had stopped stuffing the crust with mozzarella, which for some reason really pissed people off more than the fact they were eating family dust.*

Somewhere in Chinatown, a tall, black man dressed in baggy red jeans and nothing else sauntered through the market, a large boombox precariously balancing upon his shoulder. He had a cool walk about himself, a veritable skip of a walk that would leave some people thinking was cool and the rest thinking he looked a bit of a twat. Though this man didn't care, for he was high on life, and meth, and Devil's Dandruff, and West Coast Turnarounds, and Tango and Cash, and Mexican Mud, not to mention Hilary Clinton's Second Lips, Sassafras, Blue Caps, Embalming Fluid, and Ibuprofen (for he was being fairly assaulted by the mother of all headaches, and he knew not why.)

Rastafarians seldom do drugs of any kind, other than the old magic broccoli, but this man was only a part-time Rasta, and when he clocked out at 5pm, his time was his own.

Issuing forth from his boombox — which he'd just managed to retrieve from the pawn shop for the seventh time this month — was *Summer in the City* by The Lovin' Spoonful, because this is at the top of every soundtrack featuring a bustling city movie intro, or indeed intriguing and thrilling first chapter to an exemplary crime novel.

The man fluidly bounced and boogied his way through Chinatown, the music emanating from the huge device upon his shoulder drifting across the city on a light breeze. Some say it could be heard as far away as San Gabriel Valley, but those same people attesting to the hearing thereof of the aforementioned classic song had just finished having lunch with someone they would later claim was the second coming of Hitler, so who knows what to believe.

"Hey, man, what's up?" the man said to every passer-by, offering his free hand in case they wanted to slap it. Many of them didn't; some of them spat on it. It was nothing racist. His hand simply just had one of those faces that you could spit on.

Into an alleyway he disappeared, one of those dark ones whose walls were adorned with copious amounts of graffiti and whose floor was home to more used needles than the local hospital sharps deposit, more empty liquor bottles than a frat party's recycle bin, and more used condoms than an Alabama family barbecue. It was the kind of alleyway only used for certain things, by certain people, and never once as a pass-through.

Suddenly, a voice from the shadows whispered, "Pssst," which the dreadlocked man didn't hear because the music was still blasting from the boombox. It was at this moment that the man decided to switch the machine off, just as the previously unheard voice added, "Oi, dickhead!"

The Rasta turned toward the sound of the voice and grinned a mouth full of yellowing teeth. "Jay!" he said as he sauntered further into the alleyway. "My man, where yo at?"

"I'm here, Trevor," the voice whispered. "You can't see me because I'm hiding in the shadows. It's the best way to remain incognito. I'm thoroughly enjoying myself. Having a wail of a time, in fact. You should try it sometime."

"It like magic," Trevor the Rasta said, inspecting the dark alleyway, but finding no one. "Like... *black* magic. If I didn't know you were dere, I would not have suspected a ting. You should tink about going on dat show—"

"America's Got Talent!" said Jay, somewhat excitedly, though not enough to reveal his whereabouts.

"Has it?" Trevor the Rasta said. "Me hadn't noticed." He lit a thin spliff — things were very thin on the ground at the moment, so this particular spliff was made from ninety percent sawdust, eight percent dreadlock, and two percent marijuana — and said, "Anyway, me got no time for dark-alleyway shenanigans. Come out and show me the colour of yo green stuff."

"It's *green*," Jay said from somewhere or other. "Same as always." Which was not entirely true as somewhere over in Mid-Wilshire, someone — that sneaky old bastard known locally as Bobby Twoguns — had flooded the market with pink green. It was all very confusing. "But," Jay continued, "you are absolutely correct. That's enough shenanigans for one day."

Trevor the Rasta smiled. "Tank de Lord," said he. "Dis boombox ain't getting no lighter and it don't half chafe me bloodclart shoulder."

Suddenly, from the darkness, a man emerged, and he was a small man. A man no taller than half a man, and not the pretty half. Slung across one shoulder was a brown satchel, the likes of which were often seen weighing down bespectacled children outside schools. Not that Trevor the Rasta hung around outside schools; he wasn't allowed to anymore, thanks to one crying child, an extremely angry parent, and a nitpicky judge.

"Jay, my man!" exclaimed Trevor the Rasta as he danced across the dark alleyway to where the newly appeared man now stood. "You put on height?"

"New insoles," Jay said, smiling from ear to ear, which was horrible to look at because one ear was lower than the other. "Let me guess, Trev," he said, removing the satchel and riffling around its insides. "You'll be wanting the usual."

"I will, and make no mistake about it." Trevor the Rasta rubbed his hands together excitedly. Quite how he did this with the boombox still on his shoulder remains a mystery, but he did. "And... me heard dere be a little someting-someting new on de market."

Jay stopped riffling for a moment and turned his gaze toward the part-time Rastafarian. "Oh, yeah?" he said. "And what would that be?"

For the next part, Trevor the Rasta lowered his voice. "Me heard about some new magic powder called..." And he leaned in closer; Jay leaned back, just out of reach of the Rasta's rancid breath. "... clit."

It was one word, a simple one at that, but it fairly put the poker up Jay's ass. "How did you hear about the clit?" he anger-whispered. "*No one* knows about the clit! Even *I'm* not supposed to know about the clit. And even if I *did* know about it, I wouldn't know how to find it. *No* man knows how to find it, especially not me, and even if I *did* know there was a new drug out there called clit that was twice as powerful as the purest cocaine and only half the price, which I don't, I wouldn't have a *clue* how to get my hands on it, not the foggiest, so can we stop talking about the clit now? Jeez!"

Trevor the Rasta, sighed. "So you no have none?"

"I can get you some by next week, if I can find it, which I probably won't."

"My man!" And the Rastafarian fist-bumped Jay, which came as something of a surprise and so the fist caught him square in the jaw.

"Just the usual, is it then?" Jay said, rubbing at his new bruise. He produced a bag of marijuana from his brown satchel and gave it a deep sniff.

"Me got no money at de moment," Trevor the Rasta said, for he didn't, and wasn't likely to get any until his social security came through at the end of the month.

"That's a shame," Jay said, lowering the bag back into the satchel. "I'll bet that boombox is worth something to the pawn shop, if you change your mind."

"Fuck," said Trevor the Rasta. And, "Fuck!" he said again.

*

The music from the boombox — now on its way back to THE LOAN WOLF — drifts across the city once again. A tracking shot moves from left to right, high above the buildings and people (ooh, look at them! They look like ants!) and the music fades the further away it gets, which is called perdendosi and is generally what happens the further you get away from a piece of music, but that's enough of that.

The completely made-up camera tracks its way east, speeds up when it gets to Skid Row (and even then takes a brick to the lens) and shortly arrives at the 4th Street Bridge.

Now some people say that the 4th Street Bridge is not as good as the first three. Some say, as a sequel bridge, it's far too long and nothing that hasn't been done before. Many bridge-walkers simply refuse to use it as it'll never be better than the original.

Yet, if only they knew there was currently something incredibly special about the 4th Street Bridge. More specifically, the tent-dwellers currently residing underneath it. There would be queues from Pico Gardens to Boyle Heights.

The non-existent camera does a weird swoopy thing down under the bridge that would probably get a real cinematographer at least a bollocking, if not his marching orders, and zooms in on two old men standing face-to-face but at a fair old distance outside their respective tents. It is there that we join them, hopefully back in the past tense.

*

One of the men squinted (thank God for that!) painfully into the sun. The chewed, thin cigar at the corner of his mouth had gone out yesterday, but he was currently lacking in the matches department. He sighed, threw his poncho across his shoulder, and said, "You sure you want to do this, old man?" in a gravelly voice that sounded as if he'd been up all night eating pinecones.

The man facing him adjusted his Tuscan Stetson and shook a turd from the bottom of his shotgun chaps. The turd rolled across the concrete and came to a halt next to a satellite dish the man had yet to install.

"This bridge..." the second cowboy said, "... it ain't big enough for the both of us..." And he paused here before hissing, "Eastwood."

And it was! The poncho'ed man was none other than the legendary cowboy actor himself. The man with no name — although everyone that knew of said nameless man, knew that his name was Joe. Look it up if you don't believe me. Or don't. It was *the* Clint Eastwood, who now lived under the 4th Street Bridge after getting lost two weeks prior on his way home from filming his latest western epic, 'Git, or I'll Make You Git!'

"This bridge ain't big enough for the both of us," said Eastwood, "since you put up that second tent... Hackman."

And it *was*! Gene Hackman, all cowboy-ed up and ready to go. He, however, hadn't got lost; he just liked to wind the vagrant Eastwood up, even if it was costing him a fortune in camping supplies. "That's my outhouse," said Hackman.

"It's inside," Eastwood said.

"Be that as it may," Hackman said, spitting thick, black chewing tobacco to his right. It landed on the side of his horse, who whinnied and neighed and things of that general nature. "But *you* don't have an inside outhouse."

"A piss tent," Eastwood sneered, checking his cigar in case it had miraculously lit itself.

"Jealous—"

"A ur-ine stinkin', canvas water closet—"

"Fuck you!"

"Fuck you!"

"Go to hell, Eastwood!"

"Suck my balls, Hackman!"

This went on for quite some time, neither of the men moving forward, both clearly exhausted from standing still for so long, and on such a sweltering day, too! Eastwood did a little pissing down the inside of his own chaps and squinted meanly once again into the sun. Quite how the sun had gotten under the 4th Street Bridge was anyone's guess, but we'll put it down to an earlier continuity error.

"Alright, Hackman," Eastwood grunted, as was his wont. "Let's finish this once and for all." He shook out his shooting hand; arthritis was a terrible thing.

Hackman chuckled. "About damn time," said he. This was the third time this week he and Eastwood had 'finished it once and for all' and it was, Hackman thought, the funniest thing since sliced bread, or something along those lines. He almost felt guilty, coming down to the 4th Street Bridge three times a day to taunt the vagrant Eastwood, but he was having far too much fun. One of these days he would slowly help The Man with No Name back to his California mansion, but for now it was pistols at dawn once again.

"On the count of three," Eastwood said, shifting the cigarillo from one side of his mouth to the other. "One."

"Two," added Hackman.

"THREE!" said the horse.

And the former Hollywood cowboys drew their bananas at the exact same time.

*

"Everyone, tap the screen. Tap the screen. Let's get up to fifty K, yeah? Fifty K and I'll punch a passer-by in the throat, yeah? If you guys don't start sending me roses and universes and lions, I'm going to shut this live down."

The TokTiker danced in the street, her state-of-the-art phone propped up by a tripod sitting atop a trashcan. Did she care that she was blocking the sidewalk on East 10th Street? Hell no! Did it bother her that shoppers in wheelchairs were having to go off-road — or in this case on-road — to get past? Not in the slightest. As far as she was concerned, these people were getting in *her* way, preventing her from doing her job, and her job was to relieve her TokTik gifters of their hard-earned cash. It was better off in her bank account, after all, because she knew how to spend it properly on designer handbags, leather pants, expensive cosmetics and fifty-dollar coffees from boutique bistros, and luxury holidays in villas with vistas and—

"Move, bitch!" said one irate nonagenarian as she attempted to traverse the selfish young obstacle. "You kids these days with your goddamn phones and your Youtubular nonsense..." And she took to swinging her stick at the TokTiker's legs until she gave way. "Should be... in the sea... you ask me... mangy cocksuckers..." she muttered, head down and using her stick to knock aside a dead rat. She shuffled on.

The TokTiker, whose handle was BoujeeQueen27 and whose favourite food, according to her profile, was caviar on oysters, laughed loudly and rudely stuck two fingers in the air at the old bag's back.

"Can you believe how rude some people are?" BoujeeQueen27 asked her followers, of which there were many. "If I get one-hundred hearts in the next minute, I'll throw this dead rat at her," she said, and held aloft the stiff black rodent.

There were rules to being a successful TokTiker, and BoujeeQueen27 had worked her way to the top of the leaderboard by following them as if they were holy writ.

Firstly, you had to become selfish. You had to think of the money you were gifted by the naive and foolish followers not as a gift, but as an investment. They were paying her for her time, so that she might stand on street corners and dance and shout offensive things at innocent passers-by, and when they took offence at said offensive things it was great content and only made more people subscribe to her live streams, thusly making her, BoujeeQueen27, richer and richer, and so on and so forth until they had no money and she had it all—

"Why don't you get a real job, you flaxen-haired hussy?" a man shouted from the lowered window of a Honda Civic as it passed by behind her.

"*Why don't you crawl back up your mother's twat?*" screeched the TokTiker, before turning back to her viewers and offering a sweet smile. "Did you guys hear that? I don't even know what that means? Can anyone let me know in the comments what flaxen means? My God! I'm so offended by something. *Triggered* me, that has. I've been well and truly *triggered* by something or other."

The second rule of being a successful TokTiker was: keep your content fresh, and the best way to do this (according to BoujeeQueen27's unmissable YouTube series, 'How to Dupe Friends and Influence Them') was to copy someone else. Creating videos takes time, and time is money. Money makes the world go round, and the world is your oyster. Oysters are expensive, so therefore you'll need more money. It was all relatively simple according to BoujeeQueen27, but then again so was she.

"Come on, guys, tap the screen, hit those heart buttons, keep those gifts coming in, I want to see those fireworks on my screen, and remember, guys, if you're under sixteen, the best place to find your parents' credit cards is in your mother's purse."

Off in the distance there were sirens, which triggered BoujeeQueen27 even further. "I'm trying to *work* here!" she screamed in the direction of the noise. She attempted a dance move for her followers but the wailing sirens threw her off and she almost ended up in a skip behind her.

"Asshole!" a window-washer called down from above as his Bosun's chair swung side-to-side.

"You're the asshole, asshole!" BoujeeQueen27 screeched up at him. "I hope your ropes snap and you fall to your death and your children at home starve to death, and your wife dies of a broken heart—"

The sirens continued to scream on a beautiful morning in Los Angeles. Across the city a boom-box fell silent for the second time that day, a tiny drug-dealer waited patiently in a dark alleyway for a Rasta's return, and somewhere else a bananafight was reaching its conclusion.

And what was the point of all this exposition?

Just a distraction while the not-really-there intro credits ran, materialising in the air supernaturally before fading away just as quickly.

Now, onto the story proper, where the sirens—

2

"You're gonna lose the sonofabitch!" Reginald Murtow said from the passenger seat of the unmarked black Taurus. "I'm gettin' too old for this shit!"

His partner, Detective John Expendable, turned the wheel hard to the right, sideswiping an Oldsmobile being driven by an elderly man who had just recently discovered the cure for cancer and was on his way to tell the WHO all about it. The Oldsmobile plummeted into the back of a parked Honda Civic and exploded instantly. Shame, really.

"I ain't losing him!" Expendable said. "I'm just keeping my distance. He's driving recklessly." He yanked the wheel all the way to the left and took out a dawdling cyclist.

Murtow took to the radio. "Suspect heading east on Alpine Street. Chinatown. This sonofabitch doesn't look like he's gonna stop anytime soon." The radio crackled and Murtow dropped it back onto the console and tightened his grip on the dash once again.

Detective Expendable ran through two red lights, just missing a parade of vehicles coming from both left and right. Murtow made grunting noises and farted a little. At least, he hoped it was just farts. At his age — forty, pushing retirement, and far too old for this shit — every fart was risky.

Expendable sniffed and grimaced. "Just a fart?" he asked.

"I hope so," said Murtow. And then, "Look out!"

An elderly Chinese woman was crossing the street ahead. She was the owner of Won Kok, a restaurant specialising in pan-fried noodles, but Murtow and Expendable didn't know that as they barrelled toward her at breakneck speed.

"Look out for the old lady!" Murtow howled.

And then Expendable howled and at the last moment, the old woman howled, but it was all an overreaction as the Taurus drifted harmlessly past her without even knocking her glasses off.

The poor Rastafarian leaving THE LOAN WOLF and now crossing the street whilst counting newly acquired cash wasn't so lucky.

Murtow covered his eyes as the man rolled over the hood, then over the top of the Taurus. As he went, the man screamed something about, "Jus' me rarsclart luck!" but Murtow couldn't be certain he heard anything at all.

Half a dozen cruisers now followed Murtow and Expendable, sirens blazing and blue and red lights flashing. Overhead, an NBCLA news chopper followed the chase so that the people at home could enjoy it from the safety of their own sofas. The cops involved in the chase couldn't hear it, but NBC's own, Terry Moreno, was having the time of his life.

"Ladies and gentlemen, if you're just joining us, we are flying above a pursuit through the streets of LA. We've just passed over Dodger Stadium and we're now heading south toward Vernon, and my oh my! Are we having a blast with this one! There are now six cruisers in pursuit of the burgundy Honda Accord, as well as an unmarked Taurus, and so far most of the damage has been caused by the Taurus. Whatever this guy's done, it must have been bad, because these guys are just *not* giving up. We'll stick with it until its inevitable disappointing conclusion, but hopefully there will be plenty more explosions before then. Yee-haw!"

Murtow snatched up the radio again and it squawked into life. "Suspect now heading south toward the East 4th Street Bridge—"

"Oh no!" Expendable said, shaking his head. "That's my least favourite of all the bridges. Certainly not a patch on the original."

"Everyone's a critic," Murtow said as he wiped sweat from his brow. "Just keep on his ass." Into the radio he said, "And someone get rid of that damn chopper. I can hear that Moreno sonofabitch from here, and it's fairly putting me off."

"He's going off-road," Expendable said, swinging the car past and in front of a tow-truck, and he was right. The Accord was heading toward the verge which would send him on a downward trajectory to South Mission Road.

"He's trying to lose the cruisers," Murtow said. "Clever bastard."

"Well, he might lose the cruisers," said Expendable, "but he sure as hell ain't gonna lose *us*, ain't that right Murtow?"

Murtow nodded. "That's *right*," he said, and then added, "I mean, no!" But it was far too late now, and everything moved in slow motion, the way it sometimes does when cars soar high into the air, the way they often do when they leave *terra firma* at high speed.

In the three seconds they were airborne, Murtow discovered that life does not flash before your eyes just before death. The only thing that flashed before Murtow's eyes were the glove compartment and the green Little Trees air freshener as he was tossed left and right in the passenger seat. He turned to see Expendable had shut his eyes, and he was about to do the same when the car made contact with the tarmac again and they bounced about the place a bit before Expendable regained control.

Murtow was not happy with his partner, and would tell him as much later on at the precinct.

Too old for this shit, thought Murtow. And then—

"Look out for those two old cowboys with the bananas!" But it was dark underneath the East 4th Street Bridge, despite recent rumours of a sun that could penetrate steel and concrete and asphalt, and there was nothing Expendable could do as he hit both of them.

"Was that Gene Hackman?" Murtow said.

"I don't know. I was too busy focussing on Clint Eastwood."

And then Expendable hit the horse, which remarkably landed back on its hooves, seemingly unharmed.

"Must have been one of those stunt horses," Murtow said. "Like Mr Ed or Sarah Jessica-Parker."

Up ahead the Accord swung a left, back in the direction of Dodger Stadium.

The sirens were behind them now and fading; none of the cruisers had followed, and why would they? Cops weren't paid enough for heroics, and Murtow thought that Expendable had been stupid for even trying that little stunt back there. They had been lucky. *Luckier than a deaf fella at a Yoko Ono concert.*

"This chase has been going on for a bit now," Murtow said. "I'm not sure I remember what we're chasing him for."

"Nor me," said Expendable, lighting a pipe, for he was giving up cigarettes and he didn't want to look like one of those ridiculous vape arseholes. "In fact," he went on, driving over a fallen gate which had been crashed through by the Accord just moments earlier, "I'm thinking about calling the whole thing off."

Murtow considered this. He had a wife and kids at home, and he was set to retire at the end of the month. There was very little reward in all of this; letting the driver of the Accord off with whatever he was alleged to have done was somewhat appealing, if it meant he'd get home to his family in one piece. It wasn't as if the city could rescind his retirement gift: an 'Off-Duty' pint glass complete with four-piece stars-and-stripes coaster set. He was really looking forward to that.

"Oooh!" Expendable suddenly blurted. "Drugs! Something about the fella having lots of drugs in the vehicle!"

Murtow sank in his seat. "Oh, yeah," he moaned, dejected. "I remember now. Captain said it was probably an *incredible* amount of drugs." He sighed. "Millions of dollars' worth."

"And we're gonna be the ones that take that shit off the street," Expendable said with what appeared to be a second wind.

"Wonderful," Murtow muttered. "Do you think we can catch him this morning, by any chance?" he added, sarcastically. "There's probably a budget for all of this, and we don't want to peak too soon."

Expendable pushed his foot to the accelerator and the car gained speed. The distance between them and the Accord halved in less than five seconds.

Above the two cars — which now rushed across a construction site as workmen dove left and right to avoid certain death and large, heavy objects broke free of swinging cranes and crushed other, softer things below, including people — the news chopper circled.

"Can you stop circling?" Terry Moreno spoke to the pilot. "You've done it seventeen times now, ya prick, and I'm losing the will to live, and also my breakfast."

"Roger that," said the pilot, and then added, "Ya prick. Over."

Explosions began to happen all across the construction site now. Flames and smoke coiled up toward the sky. Men wearing hi-vis gear and blue helmets ran this way and that for their lives. The foreman of the site tried to calm everyone down, because it was an isolated incident — isolated to just the entire site — and that no one was getting paid if they caught fire today.

"The pursuit is now leaving what's left of a construction site and seems to be heading for the Fashion District," said Moreno. "And what do we think about those explosions, guys, huh? Didn't I tell you it was gonna be good? Damn! Almost jizzed myself! Whew!"

Meanwhile, back in the Taurus, Expendable tapped the smoked tobacco remnants from his pipe and tossed it back onto the dash. "It's now or never," he said as the pursuit returned to a pedestrianised area.

Murtow took out his six-shooter, Smith & Wesson Model 19, of course. "Get me closer," he said, leaning out through the open window.

"Use your *own* damn window!" Expendable said. "Can't see a damn thing with you draped all over me like shit on Velcro."

Murtow pushed himself back to his side of the car and out through his own open window. Up ahead, the assailant had taken to the sidewalk and now ploughed through restaurant tables and chairs with those massive umbrellas stuck in them. Morning breakfasters (as opposed to what?) either threw themselves to safety or became just another casualty. Murtow had lost count of how many civilians this guy had injured or killed; he was too busy tallying up his own score.

Left and right through the streets and avenues of the Fashion District they went. It was hotter here than a jalapeno's armpit.

"I'm going to shoot out his tyres at the next turn!" Murtow said, leaning almost entirely out of the window now. His tie flapped about his face and he accidentally pistol-whipped a lady who had apparently not seen the approaching danger in time to make a swift exit.

"Don't miss!" said Expendable, yanking the wheel hard to the left at the next junction, the same way the Accord had done moments earlier.

Tyres screeched as the Taurus struggled to maintain its grip on the road.

Reggie Murtow mumbled, "I'm too old for this shit," and then he pulled the trigger.

The car in front lurched suddenly to the right as the bullet tore through its rear tyre. It was probably hissing even now as the air rushed out of it, but everything else was far too loud to hear it if it was.

"I got it!" Murtow said, pulling himself back into the car. "I got the sonofabitch!"

And the sonofabitch had lost control of the vehicle in front and was currently swerving desperately to retake control, but it was no good, and with one final veer to the left, the car flipped, and went over and over again, obviously in ultra slow-motion, before crashing sideways into a building — INDIANA JEANS, est. 1984 — at the end of the street.

Expendable slammed on the brakes, bringing the car to a screeching halt in front of the overturned Accord, which was now doing some smoking and pissing out of radiator fluid, the way they sometimes do when they land on their roof.

Up in the NBCLA chopper, Terry Moreno reported that, "It's all over folks, but I hope that's bought some fun to your otherwise dreary lives. We return now to our scheduled show, *Inuit Ninja Warrior*."

Murtow took deep breaths; his heart was racing, and the farts in his pants, which he now knew were more than just farts, were starting to soak through to his boxers.

"You can't park there," said a traffic warden who had suddenly appeared at Murtow's window. He was already writing a ticket, the way they often do.

Murtow showed him the six-shooter and his badge, and the warden made humble apologies before heading off to annoy someone else.

Expendable was already out of the car and shouting, "Freeze!" at the motionless upside-down vehicle, his standard-issue Glock 22 sweeping over the scene of the crash, ready for any sudden movement.

Murtow exited the unmarked Taurus slowly. His back creaked, his legs cracked, his nipples honked, and his knuckles buzzed, all the regular noises you can expect to hear when you get to his age.

"Get back!" Murtow yelled at the gathering throng of nosey bastards. "LAPD," he added, showing his badge to the crowd. This only made them keener to see what was going down, and as a whole they shuffled closer, mumbling and muttering and whispering conspiratorially. Murtow had fairly had enough. "There is some AIDS in this car!" he yelled. "Everyone, get back, or the AIDS will get you!" And the surrounding crowd took quickly to their heels and screamed as they went.

Six cruisers peeled onto the scene, sirens wailing and flashing lights dancing. Uniformed officers were already cordoning off the area with yellow tape and a burger store was setting up just inside of it, because policing was extremely hungry work.

Meanwhile, Murtow approached the overturned vehicle. "Show me some hands!" he yelled, his trusty six-shooter, which was now technically a five-shooter, trained upon the broken driver's side window.

Expendable crouched and said, "You have the right to remain... oh, fuck."

"Oh, fuck, as in he's dead?" Murtow said.

"Oh, fuck, as in he's not here," Expendable said.

"Oh, fuck," said Murtow, lowering his weapon. And then he took a little looksie for himself, and then said, "Oh, fuck," one more time.

"Where the hell did he go?" Expendable said as he stood. "Did you see him run?"

"I didn't see him run."

"Maybe he got thrown out."

"Thrown out?"

"You know, when the car was going over and over in ultra slow-motion."

Murtow shook his head. "We would have seen him go," he said.

"Well, he's not here!" Expendable reiterated, and began scratching at his confused head with the barrel of his Glock 22.

"I can *see* that!" said Murtow, although he wasn't sure how he could possibly see something that wasn't there. It would probably keep him all night long. "Shit, the captain's gonna have our guts for garters," he said, whatever that meant. "And me being too old for this sh—"

Just then, an injured voice cried out. "Argh!" it said. And then, "I appear to be sandwiched between this vehicle and this wall."

It was a woman's voice. Murtow knew that because he had heard one before. He rushed around the side of the wreckage from where the voice emanated, and there he discovered a young lady, perhaps twenty or so, pinned to the wall. At least, her top half was pinned to the wall; the bottom half had unfortunately gone walkabouts.

"I'm going to go viral," she croaked, producing a smashed phone and smiling into its camera. "Yo, guys, smash that like button and hit subscribe. I've just been chopped in half and I'm with the police right now, so get gifting because new legs ain't cheap, and I'm pretty sure my vajayjay has gone to ruin, as well."

Expendable was now standing on the opposite side of the wreckage. "Hey, you're BoujeeQueen27!" he said, excitedly. "My kids love your stuff. Oh, man, they're not gonna believe this when I get home tonight. Man, what are the odds?" He took out his own phone and snapped a quick selfie with the sandwiched woman; she tried to smile for the camera, but blood was already starting to stick her lips together.

"Someone get a medic over here," Murtow called out, trying not to be sick in his mouth. He'd never seen half a person before, and all the giblets and bits and bobs hanging down from her severed torso gave him goosebumps.

Leaving the poor soon-to-be-dead woman and Detective Expendable chatting about daily rankings and photo filters and things of a general technical nature, Murtow took to his knees and began to feel around for anything drug-shaped. Moments later, his hand brushed past something hard and leathery, and now he could see it, so he grabbed the briefcase by the handle and yanked it free of the car.

"I've found the drugs," Murtow said.

"He's found the drugs," Expendable said to the dying TokTiker.

"That's... great," she managed. She turned to face her phone and her many followers. "He's found the drugs," she said, though quite why that mattered as far as she was concerned, she wasn't certain.

Murtow staggered back to the Taurus, briefcase in hand but unfortunately no perpetrator. This was going to be a hell of a day.

Once inside the car, he honked the horn to get Expendable's attention. His partner was currently getting a bloody handprint in lieu of an autograph, but when the horn startled him, he rushed toward the car at double-speed.

"Lovely girl," he said as he buckled up. He began filling his pipe with tobacco. "Shame about her bottom half, but they'll be able to sort her out at the hospital. They're good with things like that, nowadays."

"No they're not," Murtow said, trying to crack the code on the briefcase. *One-two-three-four* didn't work, as it sometimes did, so he was altogether flummoxed. It would take a crack team back at the station to figure it out. Either that or a good hammer.

"Have you tried *one-two-three-four*," Expendable said, noticing Murtow's struggle with the combination.

"Just get us back to the station," Murtow grunted. To where garters would be fashioned from guts, and a new hole would be torn where there had previously been none.

Too old for this shit, Murtow thought.
Me too, thought Expendable.

3

The precinct was bustling with activity when Murtow and Expendable entered through its automatic doors. Cops hanging around the water dispenser — which was close to the entrance — immediately stopped filling their cups and sarcastically cheered the returning detectives. One of them, a cock-eyed little rookie who must have had to buy his uniforms from fancy dress stores, said, "You guyth were amathing out there," because it wasn't bad enough he was vertically challenged, God had fucked him in the mouth department, too.

Expendable ignored the little fella as they walked past, but Murtow was far too proud to not retort. "Yeah, yeah, yeah... well, when we figure out which one of us you're talking to, we'll decide if we're offended."

Inside the precinct proper, cops all around lazed upon beanbags and perched precariously on the edges of their desks. Police scooters went this way and that across the highly-polished floor, their riders hawing and yeehing. The queue to gain admittance to the play area stretched all the way back to Interview Room 3, the one with the popcorn machine and bouncy castle. Up on the many screens hanging around the room, that morning's enthralling car chase was playing on at least six different TV channels. The ultra slow-motion bits looked the best on NBC, though.

Another cheer went up around the room when Murtow and Expendable were noticed. Hands were clapped, desks were tapped, and gunshots sounded all around as entire clips were unloaded into the ceiling. More cops, plain-clothed and uniformed, spilled into the room from the on-site casino to see what all the fuss was about.

Embarrassed, Murtow held up his hands and said, "Alright, everyone back to work. Nothing to see here."

"Yeah," Expendable added as he perused a doughnut selection box and shoved a whole one into his face. "Mph, mph mmmmm mph, mph, mm, mph," he added, which made no sense to anyone.

"Hey, Murtow!" Detective Kowalski said from the trampoline, upon which he was gaining some impressive air. "Has it ever crossed your mind that you're just..."

"TOO OLD FOR THIS SHIT!" everyone present said in unison, even Expendable, who mumbled it through his third doughnut in less than thirty seconds.

"Hey, fuck you all!" Murtow said, and he was about to continue his tirade about how they wouldn't be laughing when they were his age, how it's no fun receiving daily emails from funeral service companies enquiring as to whether he had his affairs in order — as only cheap sonsofbitches leave their wife and kids destitute when they pop their clogs — and how embarrassing it was to have to buy incontinence pads when the person working the counter is the same jackrabbit sonofabitch who lives across the street from him. He was about to say that, but...

"Oh my God, he's choking!" he of the crossed eyes and short stature said.

"No, I'm not," Murtow said. "I was just thinking of how to put it mildly."

"Not you, asshole!" Kowalski said, bouncing off the trampoline and somehow landing just in front of Murtow. "Expendable!" he said. "He's choking on his doughnut!"

Murtow spun around. And then spun around once more because he wasn't quite prepared to stop so suddenly.

His partner had turned a violent shade of red, and his eyes bulged from their sockets as if they were trying to run away. There were at least two doughnuts still in his overstuffed face; sprinkles sprayed everywhere as he coughed and choked and lurched about the place.

Kowalski patted the choking detective hard upon the back, but it did nothing to help.

"Hit him harder!" Murtow said.

Kowalski took a step back and socked Expendable square in the jaw. Bits of doughnut flew across the precinct. Officer Shaw, who suffered awfully from gluten intolerance, was yawning at the time and a bit got into her mouth. She would be lucky to see out the rest of the day alive.

"Don't hit him in the face!" Murtow bellowed. "What's he ever done to you?"

"He still owes me twenty dollars for last month's lottery!" said Kowalski. "And he was fucking my wife!"

Murtow punched Expendable in the face, which was now turning a hellish hue of Byzantium. He knew it was Byzantium because he'd just done out the guest bedroom in it.

"Somebody help him!" Kowalski screamed. "He's gone Liserian Purple!"

"Byzantium," Murtow corrected him. And then, "Everybody give me some space! I know what I'm doing! I'm going to give him the kiss of life!"

"But, he's dead, Murtow," Kowalski said, solemnly. "He died while you were double-checking that Valspar colour chart."

On the precinct floor, Detective Expendable had in fact expired. Someone was already draping Old Glory across their fallen comrade. It was the third doughnut-related death this week.

"Well ain't that just fucking great!" Kowalski said, returning to his trampoline. "I'm down twenty bucks and Murtow's down a partner." *At least I get my wife to myself again*, he thought but didn't say. He might have been angry at Expendable, but he wasn't without compassion.

Murtow couldn't believe it. His partner, gone. It just didn't bear thinking about. Expendable had had a wife and two young daughters, and unlike Kowalski's wife, Jenny Expendable would never have cheated on him. His two beautiful daughters, Page and Bookmark, would be devastated. And all because of a dry Krispy Kreme™ chocolate sprinkle doughnut. It was a tragedy. A shock and a downright bummer. Murtow didn't think he would ever get over it—

"Murtow, get your ass in my office right now!" a voice said, breaking the silence. Well, it wasn't quite silent. The springs on the trampoline were going *squeak* and *squawk* and... "Don't make me ask twice, Detective."

Murtow sighed, picked up the briefcase he'd carried into the precinct, and headed toward Captain Mahone's office. Behind him, the hubbub kicked off again, and someone let off a party-popper.

*

"I want you to meet your new partner," Mahone said as soon as Murtow entered the room. "Detective Murtow, this is Detective Marvin Ricks.

The man stood and extended a hand toward Murtow; his mullet was impressive and he looked an awful lot like he should be driving vehicles in a vast, sandy post-apocalyptic future. Murtow shook the man's hand and dusted the sand off onto his pants.

"It's a bit soon, isn't it, Captain?" Murtow said. He made a gap in the closed blinds with two fingers and peered out through it. The coroner was already on scene, and there was Jenny and Page and Bookmark. Jenny was crying over her deceased husband, but Page and Bookmark had discovered the arcade. *They will mourn later*, Murtow thought, for death was an adult's concern, and bored the hell out of anyone under fifteen.

"You have to have a partner, Murtow, you know that." Mahone slowly stalked across the office to a door, upon which there was a sign. **NEW PARTNERS**, it said in bold Comic Sans. He eased open the door to reveal a room Murtow had never seen before. Seated all around were what appeared to be cops. "These guys are just waiting for the chance to get out and kick some ass."

One of the cops, a short black guy wearing a black-and-white Detroit Lions jacket with the number 67 embroidered into its arms, said, "Hey, Mahone! I'm dying to work in Beverly Hills. Hook a brother up!"

Mahone closed the door and headed back to his desk, where he seated himself and lit a cigarette. "Shame about Expendable," he said. "He was a great detective. He will be missed. Did you know I was banging his wife?"

"Captain," Murtow said. "I don't need a new partner. Especially one with suicidal tendencies." He motioned to Ricks, who just smiled and lit a cigarette of his own.

"And how do you know Ricks is suicidal?" Mahone asked, flicking ash into an already over-filled ashtray.

Murtow pointed at Ricks. "He has rope burns around his neck and throat," he said. "And what's this?" he added, retrieving something from the seat upon which Detective Ricks had until recently been sitting. "It's a pamphlet for suicidal cops. There's a phone number here, and their motto is 'If you don't kill yourself first, our prices will finish the job!'"

"That was there when I sat down," Ricks said. "The rope burns are from kinky sex." He took a long drag on his cigarette and exhaled a plume of blue smoke into the office. Murtow couldn't even see Mahone now.

"Ricks is a damn fine detective," Mahone's voice said from somewhere amidst the fug. "A veteran. Two tours of Iraq, two tours of Afghanistan, recipient of the Medal of Honour twice, this man has more service crosses than you have pairs of glasses."

Murtow sighed. To Ricks he said, "Listen here, mullet. We do things my way. I've just lost a good partner and the last thing I need is to babysit a loose cannon. I'm retiring soon, and I've got a wife and kids—"

"*Great* wife!" Captain Mahone said, emerging from the mist like Sigourney Weaver in that film with the big monkeys.

Murtow didn't know how to take that, so he brushed it off. Besides, Tish would never cheat on him; they were solid, he and her. Nothing at all to worry about. No way, uh-uh.

"Look," Ricks said, suddenly in Murtow's face. Ricks's breath stank of cigarettes and hot-dogs and Patsy Kensit pussy. "I don't want to be hanging around with an old man all day long, either, but it looks like those are the cards we've been dealt, and if you don't like the cards then get out of the kitchen because the grass might be greener on the other side, but that's just because it always fucking rains there!"

Murtow backed off. Some of that made sense to him, but for the life of him he couldn't figure out which parts.

"Is that the drugs?" Mahone said, motioning to the briefcase in Murtow's hand. "At least you brought me something good, even if it *wasn't* the perp."

Murtow took that personally and slammed the briefcase hard down onto Mahone's desk. The house of cards at the other end toppled over, and Mahone did some grumbling before he attempted to open the case.

"What's the combination?" he asked, turning his eyes toward Murtow.

"I've tried *one-two-three-four*," Murtow said. "It didn't work. Whoever these guys are, they're really good." He shook his head. The last thing Murtow wanted in his final few weeks as a cop was to be going up against professionals.

"*Five-six-seven-eight*," Ricks said as he set about rebuilding the card house.

"What?" Mahone said.

"Try five-six-seven-eight," Ricks said with a smile. A beautiful smile it we, too. Murtow had a feeling that smile was going to grow real old real fast.

Captain Mahone fiddled with the combination, and after just a few movements of his thumbs, the case clicked open.

"Well, I'll be damned," he said, grinning. To Murtow, he said, "See, didn't I tell you he was a good detective?"

Murtow sighed. *Lucky guess*, he thought. It had to be. No one was good enough to get that right on the first go. His new partner, it seemed, was something of a fortunate bastard. *Like a deaf fella at a Yoko Ono—*

"I'll be damned," said Mahone, perusing the briefcase contents. "This is clit! This is all clit! I mean, I thought it was an urban myth, an old wives' tale, but here it is. The clit!"

"What's clit?" Murtow asked, shaking the table on purpose so that Ricks's house of cards toppled over again. It was a cunt's trick, but Murtow still didn't like the guy, even if he was good at guessing briefcase combinations.

"What's clit!" Ricks laughed.

"Ha! What's clit!" Mahone added. "Tell him, Ricks! Tell him what it is!"

Detective Ricks stopped laughing sharpish and ran his fingers nervously through his mullet. "Well, it's a... it's a..." He glanced into the open briefcase. "It's obviously some sort of washing machine powder."

"It's a *drug*!" Mahone corrected him. "Twice as potent as cocaine, half the price, and it's going to worm its way through this city until every crackhead and spice-nut is hooked."

"Now that we know what it is," Murtow said, "does that mean there will be no further running jokes about finding the clit?"

"Probably not, no," said Captain Mahone.

Just then, the office door opened a little and a head appeared. Assuming it was attached to a body, Mahone let the man explain his intrusion.

"Got some good news and bad news on the missing Eastwood case," Kowalski said, for the head belonged to him, and so, presumably, did the unseen body.

"Go on," Mahone urged him. Murtow took himself across to a corner and tried to hide behind a potted artificial Ficus.

"Well, he's no longer missing," Kowalski said.

"That's great news!" Mahone said, for he loved Clint Eastwood and every film he'd ever made, even those ones with the orangutan. "What's the bad news?"

Kowalski sighed. Murtow bristled behind the fake pot plant. "The bad news is that there's some new Clint Eastwood-shaped graffiti under the East 4th Street Bridge courtesy of this morning's pursuit."

"Goddammit, Murtow!" Mahone said, lighting another cigarette. "And get out from behind that Ficus. This ain't *Predator II*!"

Kowalski's head, along with the rest of him, probably, disappeared and the door slammed shut.

"So I'm guessing we have our first case," Ricks said, because he hadn't said a lot so far and it didn't seem fair.

"No, no," Mahone moaned, slumping back into his chair. "Eastwood's dead. Case closed."

"I meant the clit," Ricks said. "You'll be wanting us to track down the dealers, who will point us in the direction of the suppliers, which will lead us to the big businessman at the very top, who will be someone you would least expect, and then bring him to justice or probably just shoot him. That's usually how it goes in these situations, right?"

Murtow emerged sheepishly from behind the Ficus and found his place beside his new partner. He didn't like it there, so he moved across to the other side, which was much better.

"Well, that *is* usually how these things go down," Mahone said, straightening up the little sign on his desk which had his name on it, as they often do. "But be prepared, there are often little bits and bobs in-between that will confuse the plot and make getting to that final part difficult."

"Like side-quests," Murtow said, for this wasn't his first rodeo. "And there will probably be a love interest for my new partner here; some beautiful blonde associate to the bad guy at the top, and Ricks, being the blinkered, sexual bloodhound that he is, will probably fall head over heels for said woman—"

"Making things even more difficult and the plot even more convoluted." He sighed, took a long drag on his cigarette and crushed it into the overfilled ashtray.

Ricks smiled and whooped. "Best we get started then," he said. "I wouldn't mind beginning with the dirty hot blonde associate to the big bad businessman, if it's all the same to you."

"That's not how it works, Ricks," Murtow said, for this was not even his second rodeo.

"I want you to start asking around," Mahone said, picking up the fallen house of cards from his desk and shuffling them like a professional. "Someone has to know where the clit is—"

Murtow and Ricks rolled their eyes.

"—and the sooner we find it, the sooner we'll all be able to sleep at night."

Murtow said, "What about Expendable's funeral?" He would like to be there. After all, they had been partners for a long time and had saved each other's lives more times than Reggie Murtow could count on both hands—

"We've already missed it," Mahone said. "It was at noon today." He motioned to the Disney clock on the wall. Mickey Mouse's eyes went this way and that. It was five past noon. "But from what I've been told it was a lovely service, and the buffet afterwards was great."

Murtow frowned. Something seemed amiss, and yet he couldn't for the life of him think of what it might be.

To Ricks, Murtow said, "Remember, I ain't got time to babysit, so just do as I say and we'll get along just fine."

Ricks grinned, made the 'Scout's Honour" sign with two fingers, and winked at the captain, who would have noticed the wink if he hadn't been preoccupied with a jigsaw puzzle.

Murtow led his new partner out of the office, out of the station, and into the parking-lot, where the big swimming pool was. It already felt like it had been a long day, but it was only just beginning. Beside him as he walked, Detective Marvin Ricks was playing Russian Roulette with himself, his mullet swinging from side to side with every step.

This is all going to end in tragedy, Murtow thought. Just like it had for Expendable, although with a surname like that Murtow should have seen it coming.

"The pool was bigger at my last precinct," Ricks said as he climbed into Murtow's battered Taurus. "And we had a steam room/jacuzzi."

Murtow climbed in and started the car. "Just shut up, Ricks," Murtow said, and not for the last time that day. He peeled out of the dark, cool underground lot and into the bright, unforgiving heat of Los Angeles, knowing exactly who he was going to question first.

The search for the clit was on.

4

High in the sky, on the forty-fifth floor of Najatomi Heights — a building housing some of the most successful businesses in LA and its surrounding areas — sat a man. Mr. Brandt was no ordinary man; he owned everything, from Silicon Valley companies to shares in Boeing. The little girl selling lemonade out front of Najatomi Heights owed him twelve dollars in rent, and by God he would get it out of her, even if it meant hanging her upside down and giving her a jolly good shake.

Mr. Brandt, unlike some rich bastards like that Amazon whatsisname and that other guy, Elon Sprunk, had not been left a substantial inheritance by his deceased parents. In fact, he'd had them killed before they had had a chance to write a will, and seeing as neither of his parents had so much as a pot to piss in or a window to throw it out of at the time of their untimely executions, it wouldn't have made a blind bit of difference to Mr. Brandt's bank balance.

But extorting money from the little lemonade girl, whose lemonade was ersatz at best, and playing the stock markets and muscling in on failing businesses and killing anyone who got in his way, and becoming an international drug lord by the time he was thirty... *that* had led to him becoming one of the most powerful businessmen in the country.

Nay, the *world*!

He was yet to feature on the cover of TIME Magazine, but that sort of thing was not for him. That was for your

Elons and your Bozoz and your Gateses. Mr. Brandt was a force to be reckoned with, and woe betide anyone who ever attempted to take him down, and the horse they rode in on wouldn't be let off lightly, either.

Brandt was in the middle of gazing wistfully out across the city, taking in the wonderful view and watching the cars go by below like little toys (he loved to do that, Brandt did, as would anyone given half the chance) when something buzzed atop his desk.

The sudden interruption startled Mr. Brandt, and he said, "Fuck me sideways," to prove it.

He made his way across to the desk and pushed the button on the machine. "What is it, Sandra?" he said. "I was blissfully surveying the vista when you buzzed, so could you have someone send up some clean shorts?"

"It's Sherman Teague," Sandra's voice said to him through the machine. "He seems to be in a bit of a mess, sir. Could probably do with some stitches, sir. Shall I call for a doctor, sir?"

Brandt had seen the morning news, and so was already well aware of what had been going on in the streets below. He had even watched the pursuit whiz by a couple of times, going, "Wheeeee!" as it went. But now was not the time for joviality.

"Send him through," said Brandt, trying to sound as ominous as possible. "And don't forget the shorts," he added.

He made his way to the bar at the other end of the office and began to pour two glasses of whisky. Behind the bar, every type of drink you could imagine was artfully arranged in alphabetical order. It was one of those bars that has everything — little bowls of peanuts, big bowls of pretzels, sesame-glazed pistachios, all the things that made for a great social noshing. There was even a little bartender called Mac, but he must have been off changing a barrel, or something.

Yes, it was hard work as usual up on the forty-fifth floor of Najatomi Heights, and make no mistake about it. Brandt returned to the window to continue his gazing when there came a tentative knock, and then a second even more tentative knock, and then a tiny voice that said, "Oh, well, at least I tried."

"Enter," Mr. Brandt said, and then pretending to be surprised when Sherman Teague came through the door, he said, "Ah, Sherman! What brings you here on this beautiful morning?"

Sherman slowly shuffled across the carpet toward Mr. Brandt's colossal desk.

"Could you not shuffle, Sherman?" Brandt said, settling down into his gargantuan chair. "A thousand dollars per square metre, that carpet. Probably more than it costs to lino your entire kitchen."

Sherman ceased his shuffling and adopted something of a skip, as if he was terrified of even touching the carpet now. It would have been funny, had Mr. Brandt been in the mood for joviality, which he most certainly was not.

Sherman finally seated himself at the desk, and it was a desk he could barely see over, although he could just about make out the top of his employer's head, which appeared to currently be home to an angry vein. "Mister Brandt, I suppose you've already heard about the—"

"About the drugs! My drugs!" Brandt snapped suddenly. "My clit! It's been taken off your hands by the wonderful fellas down at the LAPD!"

Sherman Teague hadn't noticed the two large men entering the office behind him. He hadn't seen the thing that they had been carrying between them over their muscle-bound shoulders, and he certainly hadn't noticed them unrolling it behind him, a sheet of plastic ready for the receiving of certain fluids in order to protect the thousand dollars per square metre carpet from almost certain desecration.

"Don't mind them," Brandt said, motioning to the two burly men as they went about their business. "I'm having the ceiling redone today. I'm thinking Byzantium, for some reason."

Sherman glanced across his shoulder, saw what was happening there, and turned back to Brandt, who pushed a glass of whisky toward him. "Are you sure?" he said, nervously, "because that bit of plastic looks just about the right size for me, Mister Brandt, what with you being angry at me an—"

"Angry at you?" Brandt said. The vein on his forehead popped and a new one came through on the opposite side. It was like Whack-a-Mole. "Angry at you for losing precisely three kilos of clit, or angry at you for running amok in my city and alerting the LAPD to our goings on?"

Sherman shrugged nervously; it could have been either of those things, but was most probably, both.

"Mr. Brandt," Sherman finally mustered. His throat was drier than a nun's tasty. "Those cops they came out of nowhere. They had to have been tipped off about the drop. It's the only explanation."

Brandt finished his whisky and ordered another one from the bar, seeing as Mac had returned from the cellar. Quite how there could be a cellar in forty-fifth floor office suite was another story for another time.

"It is," Brandt said, once suitably furnished with a replenished whisky, "certainly one explanation. And yet a second comes to mind, a more realistic rationalisation."

Sherman sipped from his own glass. The whisky was warm, and so were his underpants.

"One might deduce that the LAPD had suspected you," Brandt continued, "because you saw fit to install that car of yours with a private numberplate."

"Ah," said Sherman.

"Ah, indeed," countered Brandt. "Might I ask, Mister Teague, what possessed you to purchase said numberplate? One which reads: D3A L3R?"

"D3A L3R could mean anything, Mr. Brandt," said Sherman, for it could, couldn't it? "It could mean I work at a casino... or that I trade at conventions... or..." Nope, he was all out of excuses.

"A numberplate that can be construed as meaning DEALER is hardly a smart move to make when avoiding cops," Brandt said. "In fact, one might consider it as a fucking dead giveaway."

He slammed his glass down hard on the desk and yanked open a drawer, from which he produced a shiny, black handgun. It was a Beretta M9. Sherman knew this because it was engraved along one side of the weapon.

"Don't worry about that," Brandt reassured him, for he could see the man was growing increasingly nervous. "I'm just going to give it a little clean here and there, probably unload it and give the bullets a bit of a polish. Nothing to be worried about."

"That is good to hear," Sherman said. "For a minute there I thought you were going to use it on me."

Mr. Brandt laughed. It was a villainous laugh which echoed around the room. Mac the Bartender stopped wiping glasses for a moment and the two men painting the ceiling Byzantium almost fell off their ladders.

"You have put me in quite a pickle," he said when he had finished laughing. "Clit is expensive and damn near impossible to find."

"Are we still going with that gag, sir?" Sherman asked, not because he disliked the gag, just that it might start to grow a little thin as the plot progressed.

"The old ones are the best," Brandt said, giving a bronze bullet a damn good seeing to with a monogrammed hanky.

"Yessir," Sherman said, for he was something of a 'Yes' man. As well as a 'Please don't shoot me' man, not to mention a 'I'll tell you everything you want to know' man.

"My associate, Mr. Xavier, is not going to be happy," Brandt went on. "He woke this morning, expecting to receive three kilos of the most elusive of drugs, only to find out that some twat with a giveaway numberplate had led the cops on a wild chase through LA before crashing into a brick wall."

"It wasn't just a brick wall, sir," Sherman said. "There were bits of a young woman in it."

Brandt had reassembled and reloaded the handgun, and might have been about to use it after all when his mobile phone rang and vibrated simultaneously. The second chorus of Elton John's *Rocket Man* filled the room as the phone danced its way across Brandt's desk.

He snatched it up and said, "Mister Xavier, I have already told you three times this morning that I will make good our end of the deal... yes, I know it's not good for business... I can assure you it is being dealt with as we speak..." He paused for a moment, tossed the Beretta back into the drawer and slammed it shut. "Yes, I am aware that the cops have the clit..." And then, as if he had heard something immensely satisfying, Brandt perked right up. "Oh, you do! Then send it right over."

He hung up the phone and turned his attention back to Sherman Teague, who looked relieved and yet had no clue why he should be.

"It would appear, Sherman, that I am not without good news this morning."

"It's afternoon now," one of the painters lingering behind Sherman said as he went about refilling his brush.

"Yes, well, thanks for that," Brandt said, making a mental note to have Painter 2 executed later on.

Brandt stood and walked across the office floor, signalling Sherman Teague to follow him. Sherman reluctantly did so.

A large screen began to emerge from the ceiling. Quite how that was possible on the forty-fifth floor of a—

"You were saying something about good news, Mister Brandt?" Sherman said as the screen clicked into place. It was a 92-incher. At least, that's what she said.

"I was indeed," Brandt said as he opened a window. It was one of those massive human-sized windows that buildings such as Najatomi Heights possessed. Windows that could accidentally let birds in, and even more unfortunately let humans out.

"Oh, is this the bit where you tell me not to worry? That the only reason you've opened that window is because you're going to have someone go at them with Windex and a screwed up bit of newspaper?"

"Not quite," said Brandt, and he gave Sherman Teague the gentlest of nudges and watched him stagger out through the open window, where he took to frantically flapping his arms and screaming as he fell down. There was a skip at the bottom, already filled with bodies, but from all the way up here in the sky, on the forty-fifth floor—

"Yes, we've established what floor it is," said Brandt, because if there was one thing he hated more than anything, it was needless repetition.

He listened out for the *thunk!* below, smiled, then turned his attention back to the large screen.

Upon which was now displayed the face of a balding, black man. He looked to be in his early forties; his stubble was peppered with white and his hair was seasoned with grey. His nose had been marinated in paprika and his eyes looked like they had been poached in brine. In bold white lettering beneath was the name Detective Reginald Peabody Murtow and a home address, daytime telephone number, two email addresses (one of which was 2Old4This"@copmail.com) and a list of all the schools his kids attended. It was a lengthy list, because Detective

Murtow and his wife apparently couldn't keep it in their pants.

"Murtow," Brandt said.

And that was that.

*

In the lobby of the same building, while Mr. Brandt was still looking up at the face of the detective currently in his crosshairs, a man entered. A stout, wide man was he, wearing a dirty white vest, black pants, and absolutely nothing on his feet. He limped across to the Herculean desk in the middle of the lobby and addressed the woman sitting there.

"I'm looking for Brandt Enterprises," said the man through squinted eyes. There was no reason for the squint; he just looked better with one.

The woman smiled. "That would be up on forty-five," she said. And then, "But you might want to put a tie on first."

"Thanks, ma'am," said the man, who looked an awful lot like he helped young boys who sometimes saw dead people in his spare time. He headed for the elevator, with no intention of using it the way it should be used. No, he was going to climb onto the elevator roof, shimmy up for a bit before making his way into the ventilation shafts. At some point later today, he would meet with Mr. Brandt and put a bullet in his temple, but there was no rush, not for this man, not for Jim McLeod.

"Yippee-ki-yay," said he, as the elevator doors closed.

Well, of course he did.

5

Murtow drove carefully toward Chinatown. He drove carefully *everywhere*, but that morning's excitement had fairly taken it out of him, and so he kept the vehicle at a steady twenty all the way. He could see how much it was annoying Ricks, who drummed his fingers anxiously along the dash.

"So," Murtow said, finally breaking the silence. "You're a war vet, huh. Guess we ought to register you as a lethal we—"

"Copyright, Reg," Ricks interrupted. "Have to be very careful about what we say."

Murtow was confused at first, but then it hit home. "Oh, yeah," he said. "Because of the... and the..."

Ricks nodded. His mullet, glorious as it was, went up and down. "Yeah, I saw some action," Ricks said. "I don't like to talk about it too much."

Murtow understood, and pressed no further. War was a terrible thing and could do terrible things to a man. Best not to pressure his new partner into—

"I killed eighty-six men, women, children, and other," Ricks blurted. "I guess that makes me a monster, Reg, but if I'm a monster, what does that make them?"

Murtow sighed. He didn't even know who 'them' was. *Probably the bad guys*, he thought. So then who were the 'other'? That was one he didn't want to find out.

Ricks continued. "A year in Iraq, and all I've got to show for it is this lousy tattoo." He rolled up his sleeve to reveal a picture of two girls and one cup. It must have had some meaning to Ricks, but to Murtow it meant nothing. Nice ink, though. "I've seen things, Reg. Things that'll freeze your blood."

Murtow didn't doubt it, and he suddenly felt for the poor man.

"Hey!" said Ricks. "Keep your hands to yourself."

Murtow apologised and turned his attention back to the road ahead.

"Did you know they eat dogs over there?" Ricks said, shuddering as if the thought of doing so himself repulsed him.

"In Iraq?" Murtow said. He knew they had some unhealthy habits, but that came as quite a shock to him.

"No," Ricks said. "Over there," and he pointed out the window across the bridge, to where Chinatown stood loud and proud. "Iraqis love dogs," he continued. "Love them so much they *marry* them, or so I've heard."

Murtow didn't put much stock in things he'd *heard*, but apparently Ricks was as gullible as they came. This was going to be some partnership. Like Mulder and Scully or Penn and Teller. There always had to be one rooted in the real world while the other danced off faraway with the faeries.

"I couldn't help notice your six-shooter," Ricks said, lighting a cigarette. "You fight in the civil war?"

Murtow was about to rant but choked on the smoke suddenly filling the car. "Come on, Ricks," he said. "Don't you know smoking's bad for you?"

"So's masturbating," said Ricks, zipping himself up, "but I've been going at it since we got out of the precinct, and you never said a thing."

Murtow shook his head. He *had* noticed, but thought it was just one of his new partner's rituals, perhaps something he did when he was on the way to a bust. "Just toss the cigarette," he told Ricks. "My lungs are screaming here."

Ricks did as he was told and flicked the cigarette out through the open window. It went into the open window of a passing Civic, where three young children, including a toddler whose first time it was, passed it around the backseat until it was finished.

"So, this guy we're going to see about the clit," Ricks said. "How long has he been an informant?"

"He doesn't know he *is* one yet," Murtow said.

"Ah," said Ricks. "I'm guessing he's not gonna be too happy when we show up at his door."

"Putting it lightly."

"Might even make a run for it?"

"Most likely."

"It's a good thing I'm wearing my fast sneakers," Ricks said, and he lifted one leg and showed Murtow one foot. The sneaker indeed did look fast, and if Ricks had a second on the other foot, as people so often do, Murtow thought the soon-to-be-informant had a very slim chance of taking to his own heels successfully.

"It wasn't kinky sex, was it?" Murtow asked. The question came out of nowhere. "The rope burns around your neck?"

Ricks lowered his leg and said, "Nah."

Murtow didn't know what to say. His partner was, or had been, suicidal, and had tried to hang himself in the past. *What a terrible way to go*, Murtow thought. And then he wondered how he himself would do it, if he felt low enough. Pills were the obvious choice; pain free and clean. He hated the idea of leaving a mess behind for someone else to clean up. He also hated the fact he was dwelling so deeply on something so macabre, so quickly changed the subject.

"How much wood could a woodchuck chuck if a woodchuck could chuck wood?" It wasn't the best subject change, but it would do.

"I had a woodchuck once," Ricks said, and he smiled as if in fond memory. "Killed itself, it did. Pills."

Too old for this shit.

"Reg!" Ricks suddenly yelled. "Pull over!"

Murtow's heart was already racing. "What is it?" he asked, gasping for breath that wasn't there.

But Ricks didn't answer. The car hadn't even come to a complete stop when he flung the door open and took off, across the road, to where a solitary woman stood waiting for a train on the Chinatown A-line.

6

The beautiful blonde lady was chewing gum and kicking her heels when Ricks slowly made his approach. You couldn't surprise them, he knew that. There was a certain delicateness involved when approaching a person about to take their own life, and Ricks knew better than anyone to take his time, try to talk her away from the overground tram-line before she did something she probably wouldn't live to regret.

"Hey," Ricks gently said.
The woman didn't turn around; Ricks took this a bad sign. The suicidal beauty had already made up her mind, it seemed.

"Hey, lady," Ricks said a little louder. "I know you're thinking things are bad right now, but it won't last. Things will get better. You just have to push through the negativity, and you'll come out on the other side, glad you didn't do anything stupid."

The woman slowly turned. She was mouthing something, but Ricks had no idea what it was. When she removed her earbuds, it all made sense. The woman wanted to die to a tune of her own choosing.

"Can I help you?" she said, her smile almost beatific. Ricks wished, for some reason, she would spit her chewed gum into his mouth.

"Lady, I know you're scared right now," Ricks said, holding out febrile, placatory hands. He didn't dare get any closer, for this was a woman on the very edge. One small move and over she would go, onto the tram tracks, where she would be chewed up by the next train to come along.

"I'm not scared," the woman said. The frown creasing her forehead looked like a heavy metal logo, or something. "I'll scream for help—"

"Exactly!" Ricks said, taking one risky step toward her. "This is a scream for help! A cry for help will do no good when it gets this far."

"Are you off your tits on something?" the fair-haired suicidal starlet said. She was laughing now, but it was a nervous laugh. Ricks could see she was hurting.

"Suicide is not the answer," Ricks said, moving one more step in her general direction. "There are people out there that love you. Hell, I've only known you for a minute, and I'm quite sure I love you!" The uncomfortable arrangement in his underpants suggested this was true, but now was not the time for stiffies.

The woman's nose crinkled a little. Her cheeks revealed dimples, her teeth glistened in the sunlight, and she wiped thick, dark wax from the white earbuds in her hand. It was a beautiful moment, one that Ricks would never forget for as long as he should live.

"I'm not suicidal!" gasped the woman. "I'm waiting for my train to Pacific Palisades. It should be along any minute now—"

"No!" Ricks cried, for he had only known her for the briefest of moments, and their time was already at an end. *What a world! What a fucked up world!*

"You wanna do it, huh?" he said, and now distance between him and the woman was no longer important. He moved right up beside her. Naturally, she took a few steps away. "Then I say we do it! Huh! Let's do it!"

"I don't want to do it!" said the woman, and she looked around to see if there was anyone nearby that could help her. There wasn't.

"No use changing your mind now," Ricks said. "So let's do it." He stepped onto the tracks, got to his knees, and began to lower himself onto his back. "I say we do it! I'm not letting you do it alone."

"You are a crazy man!" said the woman, and she was about to make a run for it when the man straightened back up into the vertical plane. "You are clearly a picnic short of a sandwich, or is it the other way round?" she said, "But there is something I find irresistible about you."

"Probably the mullet," said Ricks as he dusted himself down.

"Yes, that must be it," the woman replied. "My name is Velda Brugenheim. The Zee is silent."

"I didn't think I heard one," Ricks said. "Pleased to meet you, Velda. Marvin," he added, grasping her hand and giving it a good shake. "Marvin Ricks."

"No, it's *Velda*," she said, frowning once again.

Ricks laughed, Velda laughed, a passing pigeon laughed. The old ones really *were* the best.

"You thought I was going to... going to *kill* myself!" Velda said. "And you... you came to *save* me!"

"Well, it would be a shame to see such a beautiful young woman go to waste," he said, because you could say what you wanted about Marvin Ricks, and you really could, but he knew how to turn the charm on when it was necessary.

"That is so romantic," she said.

"Have you finished with your chewing gum?" Ricks said.

Just then, and not a moment too soon, the train approached from the left. It all depended on which side of the track you were standing, but for Ricks and Velda, it was definitely the left.

"Here," said Velda, and she quickly took out a business card and handed it to Ricks, who examined it.

"Very nice," he said, and went to hand it back to her.

"It has my number on it," she giggled. It was the cutest thing Ricks had ever seen. You could make a nest in those dimples, he thought.

"Great!" Ricks said. "Then, I'll definitely call that number later on, once me and my partner find the clit."

She giggled again. *God, I love her*, thought Ricks.

The train pulled to a stop, they said their goodbyes, and Velda boarded. She turned, spat her chewing gum into Ricks's gawping mouth, and the doors whispered to a close. It was a beautiful moment. Like something out of a romantic film or an exemplary action novel.

Once the train had gone, Ricks smiled and made his way back to the car. Not only had he saved that woman's life, he now had her number. Surely intercourse would follow.

"What was all that about?" Murtow asked. "How do you know that woman?"

"I think," said Ricks, "she will be the love interest working for the main baddie. She had that look about her, and she has an exotic name, *and* I'm already in love with her."

"Oh," Murtow said. "Well, at least we're getting somewhere." He put the car in gear and pulled away from the curb.

Ricks chewed the flavourless gum and smiled.

Things were ticking along nicely.

*

Ventilation shafts are dark. And warm, they are, too. It wasn't a nice place to be if it could be helped, but in Jim McLeod's case, it couldn't be helped.

He pulled himself through the shafts of Najatomi Heights like a rabid squirrel, but one ventilation shaft looks just like the next, and it wasn't until his third lap that McLeod realised he was going around in circles. Not only that, but he was still stuck on the fifth floor. The action would take place forty floors above where he now shuffled, but that was just fine. Rome wasn't built in a day, you couldn't make an omelette before cracking a few eggs, and so on and so forth.

He reached down and felt for his Zippo. It was time to strike the flint, say something witty, and then move on, but he couldn't find the lighter so instead he said, "Fuck it!" and pushed on anyway.

He couldn't rest until he was face-to-face with Brandt. The man had cost him everything, and nothing was going to get in the way of McLeod's revenge.

All of a sudden, but twice as fast, Detective Jim McLeod's head made contact with something hard and hot. "At least, that's what she said," McLeod muttered, though he didn't know why.

He was at a dead end, as in the way forward was blocked, meaning he now had to somehow shuffle backwards about two-hundred metres to the last junction. At some point during his crawling he had missed the exit.

Could always go back and take the elevator, he thought.

"No!" he said, his voice echoing around the darkness. He would not be using the elevator. for that was for too simple, and McLeod didn't do simple. He did 'hard as it can get' and he did it whilst complaining the whole way about how hard it was.

"You've got this, Jim," he said to himself as he began to reverse in the confined, unbearably humid space.

It would all be worth it in the end.

Probably.

7

Detectives Murtow and Ricks (or was it Ricks and Murtow?) took the steps up to James Toney's apartment in Chinatown. Graffiti covered the walls either side of them. Some of it was good — vibrant illustrations that could have come from the brush of Dali himself, or Magritte, or even Ernst — but most of it was telephone numbers to people's mothers who seemingly had a special on this month for anyone searching for a good time. Despite James Toney's residence sitting atop an award-winning Chinese restaurant (DONG HUNG LO) rats were running all about the place as if they paid rent. Perhaps, Murtow thought, they were running around frantically looking for a way out, lest they feature on tomorrow's specials menu.

"When we get in there, you let me do all the talking," Murtow said. "I know this guy. He might be little, and he is, but he's not stupid."

"He's all yours when we get in there, Reg," Ricks said. He was still thinking about his brief encounter with Velda

Brugenheim. He was still chewing the gum that had been in her mouth, and that was hot. At least, to him it was. *There's a fetish for everyone and everyone for a fetish*. That's what his mother used to say, and boy was she right.

Presently arriving at a filthy, splintered door, Ricks and Murtow (yes, that's definitely the way it goes) came to a halt and took out their weapons.

"Mine's bigger than yours," Murtow said.

Ricks agreed.

They put them away and took out their guns instead.

Unsure if James Toney would be armed, it was better to be prepared than to not.

"Are you ready?" Murtow asked.

Ricks finished writing a phone number on the wall next to James Toney's door, along with the message, 'For a good time, call Detective Murtow. Once you've gone black, you won't go back.'

"Where the hell did you get my number from?" Murtow asked as he frantically wiped the yet-to-dry message away with the cuff of his jacket.

"Lucky guess," Ricks said.

"Like the combination to the briefcase?" Murtow just couldn't fathom how Ricks did it, but he did, and he was damn good at it. Either that, or luckier than a deaf fella at a Yoko—

Ricks hammered at the door with the grip of his piece. It was, of course, a Beretta 92, and held fifteen rounds in the magazine. On this particular day it was home to just fourteen, as Ricks had had a bit of a bad night and put one through his fish tank before work just to let of some steam.

When no response came, Murtow hammered too. His six-shooter made little squeaking sounds as it connected with the door. Like a clown's nose, it was.

"Are you thinking what I'm thinking?" Murtow said.

"If you're thinking of creating a chewing gum that never runs out of flavour," Ricks said, "then yeah. I am."

Murtow had no idea what his partner was talking about, so decided to ignore it. "I'm thinking he's in there," he said. "He's in there, and he's ignoring the knocking."

"You're probably right, Reg," Ricks said. "Stand back."

Murtow took a step back, and then another, and another, and it was only when he grabbed onto the handrail that he managed to prevent himself from going arse over tit all the way down the stairs. He composed himself, made his way back up, and said, "Asshole," to Ricks.

Ricks gave the door a fair old boot, and on the first attempt it flew open. Murtow was amazed; it usually took him six or seven attempts to kick a door open. This kid was, as Mahone had said, a good detective.

"Freeze!" they both said, rushing into the room with their respective weapons swinging this way and that. There was a joke in there somewhere, but for the life of him, Murtow couldn't find it.

The room they now found themselves in was, as Murtow expected, more than a little unkempt. Empty bottles were strewn about the place, and Toney could have made a fortune if there was a returns reward on takeaway boxes. Flies hovered in the air, their buzzing audible even above the tumult of the streets outside. A TV which might have been manufactured at some time during the Byzantine — not the colour, for once — era displayed scenes from that morning's pursuit. The ultra slow-motion bits didn't happen because this TV had been built before the advent of special effects. No noise came from it, either, since sound hadn't been invented when this particular model rolled off the production line. The place had a certain smell about it, too. It fairly tickled at the nasal passages of both detectives.

"Smells like a decade-old wank sock in here," Ricks said, sniffing at the air. And he would know, since he had one of his own back at his hotel room.

Murtow moved deeper into the room, which didn't take long given its somewhat cubbyhole aesthetic. He didn't know the going rate for LA apartments, but if this room cost more than two dollars a month, someone — James Toney, in this case — was getting ripped off.

"Check the bathroom, Ricks," Murtow whispered as he nudged at something, possibly still alive, with the side of his shoe.

"I already did," said Ricks, holding up a half-filled cider bottle. The froth and chunks sloshing about at the top of the bottle suggested this bottle was not just for number ones.

Murtow dry-heaved, and then said, "How can anyone live like this, Ricks? I mean, damn, this guy's supposed to be a dealer. He should be living it up, not shitting in bottles."

"I guess the recession has hit us all," Ricks said, tossing the portable toilet across the room, where it hit something, and that something said, "Ow!"

And then that something was running, traversing the trash beneath its feet like a professional trash dodger. And that something was out through the door, which the detectives had carelessly left ajar upon entering, and making its way down the steps outside at haste.

"Get after him!" Murtow said, tripping over what appeared to be a mattress. Rats from within ran for cover, squeaking as they scattered this way and that. Murtow got back to his feet but was rooted to the spot by garbage. "I'll stay here and catch my breath," he said, mainly because that was all he could do. "GO!"

Ricks leapt across the room and out through the door, leaving Murtow standing there like some wheezing scarecrow.

Now, foot chases are vastly different to car chases. For one, cars tend to plough through gates and fences, willy-nilly, whereas it's much better for those on foot to go over the top of them. Ricks had found this out the hard way when he first became a cop. Also, and not least, cars find it almost impossible to scramble up the outsides of building and onto rooftops. It's just not in their nature. People on foot can also suddenly disappear into tight alleyways, whereas the laws of physics, and the width of modern-day vehicles, prevents cars from doing the same. Ricks was not much of a car chase fan, but he loved to run. He loved to run *after* things that were running away from him. It was a specialty of his, and now, with James Toney (AKA Jay the Dealer; AKA Li'l Jay; AKA The Chinchilla of Chinatown) pelting it through the streets like a rabid Usain Bolt, Ricks was in his element.

"Everyone out of the way!" Ricks cried, waving his gun around as he gave chase. People who hadn't a clue what was going on threw themselves aside, because no matter what was happening, it was best to get out of the way of a man crazily waving a gun around. No idiots, these people of Chinatown.

Up ahead, James Toney was already scaling scaffolding, which is often customary, if not mandatory, when running from the law on foot.

But that was fine with Ricks, who liked climbing things as much as he did chasing after them. He slammed into the metal poles and wooden planks at the base of the scaffolding, and, plucking the hard hat from a nearby erector (insert joke here, for I can't be bothered) he launched himself up after James Toney.

Pigeon guano, some fresh and some still warm to the taste, dripped down and around and all over the scaffolding, which made the going tough and the tough get going. Ricks almost slipped a few times, but managed to cling on by sheer willpower alone. That and his hands.

He looked skywards just in time to see the absconder pull himself over the edge of the building and presumably onto its rooftop.

"Fuck!" said Ricks, growing breathless. Perhaps it was time to spit out Velda Brugenheim's gum, for it was surely that which prevented him from swallowing air the way he normally would. But no, he couldn't get rid of the gum. It was part of her, the only part he had, and he would not be parting with it anytime soon.

With a second wind, and then a third, Ricks scampered up the scaffolding and over the top, onto the roof. He took out his gun again, having stuffed it into the back of his pants before scaling the scaffolding, even though it wasn't mentioned at the time, but that's what he had done, definitely.

It was one of those long, wide, flat roofs with bricked bits and bobs sticking up everywhere so that people trying to hide could do so. Think of that rooftop bit at the end of *The Departed*. This was just like that, but without Messrs. Damon and DiCaprio.

"I know you're up here!" Ricks called out as he slowly moved across the rooftop. "You're not in any trouble, Toney. We just want to ask you a few questions."

No reply was forthcoming. Ricks hadn't expected one.

It's a long bloody way down, Ricks thought as he glanced out and down over the side of the building. Naturally, he had the sudden urge to jump, but now wasn't the time. He had criminals to catch, powerful baddies to ensnare, blonde beauties to ravish, and, all of a sudden and most regrettably, a bladder to empty.

That was when something hit him.

It was, he would later discover, a two-by-four, and it caught him right at the back of the head where the soft bit was. Had it not been for his magnificent mullet, and the hard hat which flew off and skittered across the rooftop, it would have hurt like a sonofabitch.

Still, and despite the haircut both favoured and worshipped by Mississippi miners (and that's just the women!) Ricks went down and rolled across the concrete rooftop. He was quick to his feet, though, and turned just in time to block a second attack from the plank, at the other end of which was James Toney.

Ricks threw a jab to the ribs of the little dealer, which was something of an achievement in itself given how close to the floor they were, and James Toney grunted as air evacuated his lungs. He had, Ricks thought, the breath of a water-starved camel, but it would have been rude to tell him so.

"Why run?" Ricks asked the dealer, who was now doubled over and sucking in great big lungfuls of Chinatown air.

"You... you were in... you were in my *place*, man!" He suddenly straightened and threw a little leg toward Ricks, who parried it easily before dealing another jab to the dealer, this time to the temple.

"Almost didn't see you hiding in your place," Ricks said. "If you hadn't gone 'uh!' when that portable toilet hit you, we'd have been none the wiser."

"I've been practising my hiding skills," said James Toney. "It's difficult when it ain't a dark, shadowy alleyway. Clearly need to work on 'em."

"We're not after you," Ricks said, although at this point he didn't know who they *were* after; Murtow hadn't told him much of anything. "We're after the clit!" he said. "And whoever currently has it."

Rubbing at his head, and drooling like Denzel during the King Kong monologue of *Training Day*, James Toney said, "Man, I don't know *nothing* about no clit. Last I heard it was mythical, like that flying horse or that bitch with the snakes on her head." He threw two punches in Ricks's general direction, but Ricks had already placed his palm on James Toney's forehead and was holding him at arm's length as the dealer continued to swing wildly.

"Let me tell you," Ricks said, releasing the man but keeping his gun on him. "The clit is real. I've seen it for myself, and we need to know where it's coming from and who's supplying it to assholes like you."

James Toney shrugged. "I don't know *nothing*, man," he said, which was true. His own mother had told him so growing up. "You've got the wrong guy. All I've got is weed, and I can't even vouch for the efficacy of *that*." He didn't, as his mother had told him growing up, know nothing, except the meaning of the word 'efficacy', and he'd been dying to use it someday, and now that he had he could tell his mama to go f—

"Hey, Ricks," a breathless voice said.

Ricks turned to find Murtow breathlessly pulling himself onto the rooftop. "Oh, hey, Reg," Ricks said. "Your informant here says he don't know nothing about nothing."

"That's probably true," Murtow said. His six-shooter now joined Ricks's Beretta in pointing at the dealer. "I knew his mother, and she always said he was knowledge impaired."

"What does that even *mean*?" James Toney (AKA Tomfool Toney; AKA Momma's Second Favourite James, after James Ritchie, the serial killer) asked.

"See what I mean?" said Murtow. "But my partner and I need to cross your name off our list, eliminate you from the investigation, so to speak."

James Toney held his hands up, which is probably the best thing to do when threatened with not one but two guns. "Without sounding like a broken record," he said, "I know nothing of the clit." He enunciated each syllable as if the detectives were the dumb ones, which is the very last thing you should do when threatened with not one but two guns.

Murtow looked at Ricks.

Ricks looked at Murtow.

James Toney looked at both of them at the same time, which was quite the feat as they were standing ten feet apart, and also played havoc with his eyeballs.

"Cuff him, Ricks," Murtow said, lowering his weapon. "We're gonna have to take him in."

"I seem to be a little light in the cuffs department," Ricks said, feeling around his waist at the nothingness that was there. "Why don't *you* cuff him, and I'll watch for next time?"

Murtow sighed, produced a shiny pair of steel bracelets, and set about cuffing James Toney. "You have the right to remain silent," he said. "Anything you say can and will be used against you in a court of—"

James Toney began to cry.

*

The interrogation room was exactly as one might imagine; very little in the way of creature comforts. A desk sat in the middle, with a chair on either side. The two-way mirror, which was fooling absolutely no one, not even James Toney, took up the majority of the wall in front of him. The candy-floss machine was out of order, according to the sign, and the juggling midgets were told to take a hike as soon as the room became occupied. A light dangled directly above the desk, its five-hundred-watt bulb more menacing now that the shadow-puppet fella had left with the midgets.

James Toney (let's just call him Jay from now on to save on printer ink) sat alone at the desk, staring at himself in the two-way mirror. He was no longer cuffed, but the cameras pointing down at him from each corner of the room suggested he'd be a fool to do anything stupid. He was about to put his head down for a nap when the door flew open and in walked the one with the mullet and quasi-Australian accent.

"Well, I guess it's just the two of us," Ricks said. He dropped a folder down on the desk and took his seat. "Do you mind if I call you Jay?" he asked. "It's better for the environment."

Jay shrugged. "Call me whatever you want, man, but I still ain't gonna be able to help you."

Ricks opened the folder. It was empty, and only there for dramatic effect, so he quickly shut it again.

"Quite a record you have." Ricks stood again. The chair was not in the least bit comfy. "Ten counts of possession with intent to supply. Twenty-eight counts of possession with intent to smoke yourself, and one count of possession by demon which, had it not been for the Vatican, your head would be spinning like a ballerina in Hell by now."

"That last one wasn't my fault—"

"Two years in jail for pimping, three years in jail for armed robbery, six months for battery, and six months for vomiting on a priest." Ricks whistled. "You're looking at the chair," said he.

"It's because it doesn't look very comfy," Jay said, because it didn't, and it wasn't.

Ricks clipped Jay around the earhole. "Smart man, huh? You're gonna fry for this." And to prove just how angry he was, he gave Jay's nipple a very violent tweak.

Jay squeaked. He was about to scream bloody murder when the door flew open again and in came Murtow.

"Hey!" said Murtow to Ricks. "You can't do that to a suspect. That's ever so naughty, that is. Why don't you go outside, cool off, get your shit together, and come back when you're going to play nicely."

Ricks shook his head angrily, but backed into a corner. And in the corner he remained as Murtow wheeled in a trolley, and upon said trolley was one of the best spreads ever put together. There were cheeses, and artisan breads; countless pastries and meats; three pickle potato salads and a peach cobbler. There was also a bottle of red wine, but Murtow had forgotten the corkscrew.

"You want something to eat, Jay?" Murtow said as he began to build himself a sandwich from the heavenly array of fresh goods. "Tell us what you know and you can help yourself."

"I see what you're doing," Jay said. "Good cop, bad cop, am I right?"

Ricks walked across the room and cuffed Jay about the temple. Murtow put a band-aid on it.

"Good cop bad... I've never *heard* of that," Murtow said, hoping his evening classes at Am-Dram were finally paying off. "You should really try some of this caviar," he added, dipping a finger into the roe and sucking it off (ahem).

"That does look good," Jay said, and then quickly added, "the caviar... I meant the caviar, not... not the way you sucked it off."

In the corner, which was where he had returned to, Ricks shuddered. They were getting nowhere fast.

"He knows where the clit is!" Ricks said, and he came out of the corner to poke Jay in the eye. Then he did the other eye, as well.

"Fuck!" said Jay, blinking and rubbing and blinking again.

"Oh, man," Murtow said, applying eye-drops to the victim. "That looked like it hurt. Here," he said, offering Jay two thin slices of cucumber from the trolley. "It works for my wife."

"Okay, okay, okay!" Jay said. "I'll tell you what I know, but it ain't a lot."

Murtow smiled at Ricks.

Ricks smiled at Murtow.

Jay didn't see this subtle exchange between the detectives; he couldn't see anything at *all* through the cucumber slices.

"There's this guy. Xavier. Don't know his first name, and I don't wanna know. I've never met him, so I don't know what he looks like, but he's the guy I buy from."

"Who's your go-between?" Ricks asked, eating a handful of grapes off the trolley.

"Just a henchman," Jay said. "Nondescript. Wouldn't know him from Adam, that sort of fella."

Ricks went to hit him again.

"Okay, okay, okay!" Jay said, for the cucumber slices had slid off his face. "This Xavier, he's got a mansion in Pacific Palisades. One of those big whatchamacallits with the sixty-foot swimming pools and the ladies in the bikinis dancing around to Prince and sniffing coke all day while nondescript henchmen guard the property and all that malarkey."

Pacific Palisades, Ricks thought. That's where Velda Brugenheim—*his* Velda Brugenheim—had been headed to on her train. What were the odds? Pretty damn good, considering she was probably working for the man at the top, the main villain, the big cheese.

"Here," Ricks said, and he tossed Jay a Cheez-It and a permanent marker. "Write the address down."

"I have to tell you, man," Jay said, struggling to get the marker working on the cracker, "you guys don't know who you're going up against. Xavier's a sick sonofabitch. I heard he once threw someone out of a four-storey window just because he gave Xavier's girlfriend a foot massage." The marker still wasn't taking to the Cheez-It. "This cracker's a pain in the ass!" he said.

Ricks kicked him in the shin before realising Jay meant the Cheez-It, and not him, the only white man in the room.

Murtow handed Jay a lettuce leaf, which seemed to do the job.

"See?" Ricks said once the address was written down. "That wasn't so hard, was it?" He winked at Jay. "You're free to go."

"Don't let the door hit you in the ass on the way out," Murtow added.

"You guys suck," Jay said, and he stood up and took his leave.

The door hit him in the ass on the way out.

"So, we go after Mister Xavier, right?" Murtow gnawed on a celery stick.

"Sounds like a plan." Ricks fingered a Bakewell tart. "We really are getting quite a lot done in one day, don't you think?"

"I thought that, yeah."

"It's almost like time is different here. I mean, with your car chase this morning, then us partnering up, me meeting

79

the beautiful suicide blonde who's definitely going to play a part in this caper later on, and then that foot chase."

"I'm a bit knackered already," Murtow said.

"And me," said Ricks, shaking out his limbs. "And, I'm not gonna lie, my jaw is giving me some right gyp with this chewing gum."

"Hm," said Murtow, pondering this. "What time is it now?"

Ricks looked at his watch, sighed deeply, and said, "It's only half past one."

"Ridiculous," Murtow said.

Indeed it was.

8

Detective Jim McLeod, NYPD cop in LA, was about to give up crawling through the dark ventilation shafts on the fifth floor Of Najatomi Heights when he heard something up ahead. It was a voice. A whispering voice. And it whispered, "Is there someone in here?"

"Who's that?" asked McLeod. "Is that you, God?"

"No," whispered the voice. "It's Mervin. I'm the janitor. Are you stuck?"

McLeod thought about this, decided that he was, and said, "Yeah. I thought I'd be alright, but these shafts are tighter than they look."

"They always are," whispered Mervin the janitor. "What hell are you doing crawling through the vents anyway?"

"Making my way up to forty-five," McLeod whispered back. And then, realising what a dickhead he was, he added, "Why are we whispering?"

"I don't know," Mervin said. "I thought you were a big rat, and I didn't want to startle you."

Big rat, McLeod thought. And also, *cheeky fucker*.

"Don't go anywhere," McLeod said. "I'm coming to you. Just keep making noises so I know where you are."

Mervin sighed, muttered something about silly buggers that McLeod didn't quite catch, and then started to sing the first verse of *Single Ladies* by Beyonce. "Now put your hands up. Up in the club, we just broke up, I'm doing my own little—"

"Don't you know anything else?" McLeod said as he shuffled through the darkness toward the source of the racket.

"I know *Barbie Girl* by Aqua," Mervin said, and then set about murdering that one, also.

"Just... just keep talking to me," McLeod said. He could bear no further singing. Besides, he was getting close now. He could see a block of light up ahead, and a head, there was, sticking up through it.

"I see you," Mervin the janitor said. "Hey... this is like that bit in Aliens. Do you want me to make beeping noises like the space marines' motion trackers.

"No!" McLeod said. "I'll be out in a minute." Slowly he shuffled forward, and Mervin's head became clearer. It was a funny looking head, with big, bushy eyebrows and a pussy-tickler moustache. He had one ear bigger than other, which was why his glasses were all skew-whiff across his face. He had a face for radio—or a face that had been beaten repeatedly by a radio—but apart from that, he was a real looker. McLeod was sure his mother loved him.

"Here, let me help you," Mervin said when McLeod was within touching distance, and help him he did, down into what appeared to be a broom cupboard.

"Bit of a tight fit in here," McLeod said, dusting himself off. "One of us should take a pregnancy test as soon as possible."

"So," Mervin said, moving carefully around McLeod so as not to rub him up the wrong way, or rub him in any way at all. "What's up on forty-five?" he said.

"The man who took everything me," McLeod said, and he screwed his face up to show how much the man who had taken everything from him, and was now up on forty-five, disgusted him.

"Please don't do that again," Mervin said about the screwed-up face. "It's terribly off-putting."

"I'm a cop, Marvin—"

"Mervin."

"I'm a cop, *Mervin*. An NYPD cop come to LA to put a bullet through the man who stole my wife."

"He *stole* your wife." Mervin didn't know much about wives—having never married, himself—or the stealing thereof, but he knew that it usually took two to Tango, and one to do the robot. You could usually pull off a pretty decent Rumba with three people, but the YMCA needed four, no more, no less, otherwise you'd only be able to spell out the words *MAY* or *YAM* or—

"He *manipulated* her, Marcus—"

"Mervin."

"He manipulated her, *Mervin*, and convinced her to leave me, but not before getting her to invest all of our money in one of his fake companies. It was a lot of money, Merv. And once he had fucked my wife, and stolen our money, and adopted our two children and then sold them on to traffickers, and put my dog in the canal—"

"He put your dog in the canal?" Mervin looked as if his flabber had been truly gasted. "Sick sonofabitch!"

"*Exactly*, Mervin, so you see, I had to come all the way out here to finish this Mr. Brandt once and for all, before he does the terrible same to someone else."

"And you didn't think to bring a gun to put a bullet in this man, this Brandt's, phizzog?"

"Have you ever tried to get a gun through customs, Merrily-We-Roll-Along?"

"It's *Mervin*," said the janitor once again. "And I've never been through customs before. Is it bad, is it?"

Detective Jim McLeod of the NYPD rolled his eyes and clucked his tongue. He also yanked his chain and blossomed his arsehole (which Elvis Presley would have loved, had he been there, which he wasn't so he didn't).

"It's a *nightmare*, Mervin. The best thing to do, I thought, was get here first, and worry about weapons and plans and things of that nature when the time arose."

"Which brings me nicely to what you're wearing," said Mervin, and he waved a calloused hand all and around McLeod's body. "Or in your case, *not* wearing."

"The dirty, bloody white vest?" McLeod asked, tugging at the same. He was starting to like Maybe-it's-Maybelline. "This old thing has seen me through some tough times," he went on. "It's my lucky vest."

"It doesn't *look* very lucky," Mervin said. "It's got more holes in it than a women-only orgy in a Swiss cheese factory."

"Bullet holes, Mandela," said McLeod. The janitor thought about correcting him, but could no longer be bothered. "I've taken down German terrorists more times than you've had hot dinners, and rescued more hostages than you've had cold suppers. I've had dalliances with British baddies, fumblances with French foes, run-ins with Russian rascals, and more proceedings with Polish prats than you've had painful pisses." The alliteration was starting to, like his lucky white vest, wear a bit thin

"And what's the barefoot thing all about?" Mervin asked. "You don't strike me as a Sandy Shaw fan."

"I have a fetish," McLeod said. "Love feet more than Tarantino loves feet, I do. Especially my own feet; can't get enough of them. If you sit on them just right, you can get your big toe right up inside yourself. If you were to ask me to choose between losing my feet and losing my arms, I'd tell you to lop my arms off, no problem." He frowned a little, for it had all sounded so sane in his head, yet clearly it wasn't and he was as mad as a March hare.

Mervin also frowned, so suddenly that his skew-whiff glasses fell off the end of his nose. "So how come," he said, "you're scurrying around in the vents on the fifth floor, instead of up there on forty-five putting an end to Mister Brandt?"

"I like to make things interesting," said McLeod. "I could have gone straight up in the elevator, but where's the fun in that?"

Mervin the janitor didn't know where the fun was in *any* of this, but he was sure *someone* would buy it and eat it all up without question.

"A man of action, I am," McLeod said, somewhat proudly. "So I do crawlings through things, and climbings on top of things, and swingings from things. Eventually, and once I've done all of that stuff, I'll end up doing the shootings of main baddies. That's the way I've always done it. Oh, and I've never needed a partner to do it, either. No way, José. I'm a man who gets things done on his own, an NYPD cop on a solo mission—"

"But you're *not*, though, are you?" Mervin picked up his glasses and put them back on his face. Neither of them said anything of the accidental nudge of janitor's head to cop's groin in the confined space of wherever they were; why on earth would they?

"Not *what*?" McLeod said.

"Not getting things done. The only thing you've managed to do is stop me from getting *my* job done, which is to fix the door to BLASÉ BANKING PLC. It's terribly squeaky, you see, about the hinge department, and clients keep thinking there are mice afoot."

"Yeah, you're right, I should probably get back to work myself." McLeod manoeuvred around the janitor, standing between him and the corridor beyond the tiny broom cupboard. "Before I go," he said to Moonpigdotcom, "does this building have a freight elevator I could borrow for a bit? I've given up on the vents for now."

9

"Well, this is all a bit fancy, ain't it?"

Ricks had seen mansions before. Had even broken into one when he was a kid, but that was another tale for another book. Perhaps an origin story or—

"Imagine living like this," Murtow said, driving slowly past one of the huge buildings. There were big white pillars out front and it had plenty of parking space with easy access to hiking paths. Breathtaking ocean vistas could be observed from any of its twenty-six bedroom windows, and all this in a city famous for its diversity and—

"Can you not do that, Reg?" Ricks said.

"Sorry," Murtow apologised. "I do it sometimes just before a bust. It relaxes me. I don't even know I'm doing it, truth be told. Like what geriatric nuns wear, it's an old habit."

Is that the kind of joke we're running with now, Ricks thought. *We're not even halfway through*.

The car climbed slowly up a hill. The biggest of all houses, a veritable McMansion, if you will, stood at the top, gazing down over the wonderful scenery below. Beautiful green hillocks on all sides, you would be crazy not to live in any one of these stunning—

"You're doing it again," said Ricks, and this time he gave his partner a gentle cuff about the lughole.

Murtow made verbal protestations, but Ricks wasn't interested. He was too busy thinking about Velda Brugenheim, his beau, and how she had managed to get herself all tied up in this. He was also thinking of his poor jaw, and the gum he still chewed at—a parting gift from Velda, spat affectionately into his mouth as he stood watching her leave from the platform in Chinatown—that would last him all the way through to this mission's no doubt brutal and violent denouement.

"Even the sun is hotter up here," Murtow said, fiddling with his shirt collar. "It's like it knows this is where the money's at, and it's just showing off."

"Can you hear that?" Ricks said as Murtow slowed the battered Taurus at the top of the hill in front of the mansion.

"Yeah, I hear it," Murtow said. Because he could.

It sounded like girls. Lots of girls frolicking and whooping and splashing about in a pool yet to be seen by the detectives. "You can't put that in there!" one of the girls, also yet to be seen, playfully screeched. "I'm a Catholic!"

Murtow parked the car next to a Bentley, and it was a Bentley that didn't have dents in it, and its windscreen wasn't all spiderwebbed with cracks.

"Tish is going to kick my ass when she sees what I've done to the car," he said.

"Oh, yeah, I almost forgot you were married," Ricks said, making sure his Beretta was fully-loaded. "And how many kids you got?" he added as an afterthought. He didn't care, really. Once you've had one kid, you've had them all.

"Four, I think," Murtow said. He did some counting upon his fingers before correcting himself. "Seven!"

They climbed out of the car and slammed their respective doors. The one on Ricks's side fell off.

"What time is it?" Ricks asked.

Murtow looked at his watch, saw that the big hand was on the six and the little hand was between one and two. "It's half past one," he said.

"Still?" Ricks didn't know how that was possible. Time truly was a mystery.

"Well, if this shit goes south," Murtow said, "tell my wife and kids I love them."

"Tell 'em yourself," said Ricks. "I can't be bothered."

They walked slowly and deliberately across the gravelled driveway toward the side of the mansion, where a beautiful Casa Padrino stone fountain sprayed water upwards and a generously-breasted stone woman stood gazing solemnly off into the distance and—

"Knock it off!" Ricks said, nudging Murtow. "Do you have any idea how annoying that is?"

"Can I just finish this one?" said Murtow. "I was almost at the end."

Ricks sighed, stopped walking for a moment and admired the fountain. "Go on, then," he said. "But no more after this."

Murtow nodded. He understood. "And standing at the side of this wonderful baroque creation, featuring excellent workmanship and easy care and durable materials, we see a little boy pissing."

"Better?" Ricks said, and, *What a terribly strange affectation*, he thought.

"Much better," Murtow said.

They continued walking, made their way carefully along the side of the mansion. Straight in front there was a large, golden-finialled double-gate—Ricks made eyes at Murtow which said, "Don't you dare!"—and standing like Roman Gods in front of the gate were what appeared to be two doormen.

"Hey, guys! We're here for the party!" Ricks said, tucking his gun into the band of his jeans. He moved toward the guardians of the gate as if they were old friends of his. "Sounds like a blast in there!"

"Yeah, yeah, the party," Murtow said, his Smith & Wesson already holstered and hidden from view beneath his blazer. "Sounds... sounds like those girls in there are having some fun, huh?"

"And we're here to join in!" Ricks said. He was within punching distance of the doormen now, though he didn't fancy being punched by either of them, for they were fucking massive, with fists as big as his head and noses that had been broken so many times, they could hardly be called noses anymore.

"This party is invite only," the one on the left said. Well, it all depended on which side of the gate you were, but from where Ricks and Murtow were, it was the one on the left.

"Of course!" Ricks said, looking from one giant man to the other. "Who comes to a party they're not invited to?"

"You would be surprised," the one on the right said, and he said it with more than a hint of a Russian accent. "There are some very crazy people out there."

Ricks took a slight step back, away from the Russian, for he didn't like the way Vladisvar was looking at him.

"Well, we're not crazy," Murtow said. "Mister Xavier invited us personally."

Ricks looked at Murtow.

Murtow looked at Ricks.

The doormen looked at both of them.

"Xavier invited you?" said the fella on the left, who definitely wasn't Russian, but what he was would never be known as he, along with Vladisvar, was only integral to this small part of the plot and therefore would not feature later on when it *really* kicked in. Even his own mother didn't love him.

"Yeah," Ricks said, suddenly excitable again. "Xavier called us up this morning, told us to swing by, said there would be girls of the scantily-clad variety frolicking both next to and also in the pool and that there would be a buffet of free drugs, as well as asparagus tips."

"I do like asparagus tips," said the Russian with a smile.

"Okay," the one on the left said, and he eased open the gate and stood aside. "In you go. Enjoy yourselves, but keep your hands to yourself, and steer clear of the devilled eggs."

Ricks and Murtow entered, thanking the giant doormen profusely as they passed.

"Nice fellas," Ricks said. "Hope we don't have to shoot them in a bit when it all goes tits up."

The party at the rear of the mansion was a sight to behold, so behold it they did. "This is something else!" Ricks said, though if it was not what it was supposed to be—a drug-fuelled jamboree with near-naked girls prancing all about the place and playing keepy-uppy with an oversized beach ball whilst under the influence of various illegal substances, including the devilled eggs, apparently—then what the hell was it?

Ricks was about to announce his arrival to the prancing girls and the swimming pool when Murtow took him roughly by the arm.

"Try to remember why we're here," Murtow said.

"I'm trying," Ricks said, "but it's awfully hard."

"I can see that," said Murtow, gesticulating to Rick's jeans frontage and the protrusion therein.

Ricks quickly rearranged himself and smiled sheepishly. "What can I say?" he said. "I'm a hot-blooded singleton," though that wasn't quite true. He and Velda Brugenheim were practically as married as Murtow and Tish. He had her gum to prove it.

"Let's find Xavier so we can get the fuck out of here." Murtow walked toward the mansion, more specifically the side-door leading into it. Ricks limped after him.

Inside was just as impressive as outside. The kitchen cabinetry had been ergonomically tailored by a master craftsman who had trained for a decade, and the brushed gold Cubo undermount double kitchen sink—

"Ouch!" Murtow rubbed at his shin, which had just taken a kick. "Was I doing it again?"

"You were," Ricks said as he riffled through the kitchen drawers. "Oh, look!" he said. "It just goes to show, no matter how much money you've got, you will always have a kitchen junk drawer."

Murtow leaned in to take a look, and saw that Ricks was right. Within the drawer there were loose batteries that might or might not work and biros with varying levels of ink. There were those little candles you stick in birthday cakes and rubber bands, thumbtacks and tiny tools which had been won from Christmas crackers, takeout menus and bendable straws, old phones and cables to electronics no longer possessed, random little keys (is this for a window?) and leftover Ikea fixings, coins and notes in currencies no longer legal and one of those long yellow tape measures all knotted up. This was definitely a kitchen junk drawer.

Ricks slid it shut, but not before helping himself to the loose batteries. "You can never have enough batteries," he said. "And even if they're dead, pop them in your TV remote, they'll work for at least a year."

"Can I help you gentlemen?" The voice was deep. Baritone, Ricks thought. He turned to see Mister Xavier, for it had to be; he was wearing a big blue badge bearing the words "Birthday Boy". His big bald bonce bore a *Breaking*

Benjamin tattoo. Between his bright blue eyes there was a bloody big boil, 'bout to burst. Alliteration aside, because that gag was used in the last chapter, to very little fanfare, Xavier looked like a man not to be messed with.

"You must be Xavier," Murtow said.

"You must be the brave boys in blue 'bout to bust—"

"We've stopped doing that now," Ricks said.

"Good," Xavier replied. "It *was* getting a little tedious."

Grinning, Ricks walked around the island in the middle of the kitchen. It took him almost five minutes, but somehow, when Murtow checked his watch, it was only one-thirty-two.

"We had a little chat earlier," Ricks said, finally reaching the other side of the island, "with a friend of yours."

"I have no friends," Xavier said. "Just business associates and those noisy, naughty nookie-nymphs nearby." He nodded; that was a good one.

"Aw, James Toney will be sad to hear that you don't consider him a buddy," Ricks said. "He tried to cover for you at first, but I guess you're right. You really do have an absence of friends."

"Yes, well, the thing with people is that they are loyal only to a certain point. Which is why you are here now, am I right, gentlemen?"

"Actually," Murtow said, "We're here to give your drug buffet a once over. We're looking for a new kid on the block, twice as potent as cocaine for half the price. We're looking for the clit."

"The clit is a myth!" Xavier laughed, and it was one of those villainous laughs made famous by the likes of Charles Dance and Alan Rickman and Joss Ackland. It put the shits right up Murtow, but Ricks didn't seem affected by it. "It doesn't exist, detectives."

"Then how come I found it just this morning?" Murtow smiled when Xavier's face dropped. He picked it back up, but Murtow had certainly got to him. "That's right," he went on. "I might be too old for this shit, but I ain't too old to find the clit."

Ricks laughed.

Murtow laughed.

Mister Xavier did not. He was down precisely three kilos of clit, had fallen out with Brandt because of it, had had that idiot Sherman Teague thrown from a forty-fifth-floor window for his failure; what was there to laugh about? He didn't know when he would be reimbursed, or if indeed he would be at all. *And* he'd been looking forward to sampling some clit all night long, before putting it officially out onto the streets.

Just then, a beautiful blonde babe entered the room behind Xavier. It was Velda Brugenheim, and when she saw Ricks standing there in front of Mr Xavier, she looked both dazed and confused.

"Ah, Ms. Brugenheim!" Xavier said, jollily. "All done, are they?"

Ricks thought she looked uncomfortable, but just as beautiful as the day he met her. Which was still today. In fact, it was less than an hour ago, but by God she hadn't changed a bit.

"Yes, Mister Xavier," said she. "Your accounts are all up-to-date, so I'll be on my way." And she made for the exit.

"I'll call you later, Velda!" Ricks said. And then, "I still have your gum in my gob!" but she was already gone, the sound of a door slamming shut seemingly punctuating her exit stage right.

"Oh," Xavier said. "Do you and Ms. Brugenheim know each other, copper?"

Ricks turned to Murtow, who did furtive shakings of his head. Turning back to Xavier, Ricks said, "No. I'm just really good at guessing first names. You said she was Ms. Brugenheim. The only first name that goes with that is Velda."

"He *is* really good at it," Murtow said. "He knew my name was Reginald before we even met, ain't that right, Ricks?"

"Yeah, that's right," Ricks said, twirling his stunning mullet curls and trying not to make eye-contact with Xavier.

"Then what's my first name, Detective Ricks?" Xavier said.

"Hm?"

"What, if you are so good at guessing first names, is mine, Detective?"

Ricks looked at Murtow.

Murtow looked at the near-naked ladies out by the pool.

Xavier looked pleased with himself.

"Percival!" Ricks suddenly said.

"What?"

"Your first name, it's Percival."

"That's impossible!" Xavier said. "No one knows my first name. Not even the FBI. That was a lucky guess!"

Murtow looked just as shocked as Ricks and Xavier. *Man, he is a great detective*, he thought. And then also, *We'd better get the fuck out of here before his luck runs out.*

"And on that surprising note," Murtow said, "we'll be taking our leave." He waited for Ricks to join him back on his side of the kitchen island before adding, "We'll be keeping a close eye on you, *Percival*. You and your clit."

Once they were outside and clear of the mansion, Murtow pulled Ricks to a halt. "How?" he said. "How in the hell did you know his first name was Percival?"

Ricks tapped at his nose and smiled. "I'm just a great detective," he said. "Oh, and it was printed on his big blue birthday badge."

10

Ricks called the number on the business card Velda had given to him and waited for an answer. To Murtow, who was driving slowly and avoiding bumps and potholes so that no further bits fell off the car, he said, "What time is it now?"

"Almost three," Murtow said.

"Thank fuck for that. I thought we were stuck in time... hello, Velda! Sweetheart! It's Marvin Ricks, from earlier at the train stop, and then again at the Xavier McMansion... yeah, I know it was a bit awkward, wasn't it? Yeah, yeah, yeah. Uh-huh. Yeah. Yup. Actually, we were there looking for clit. but it turns out he hasn't got any at the moment, so we couldn't bust him... no, no, *yeah*, I *know*, right? Anyway, I was wondering if you would like to go out to dinner tonight, somewhere cheap because I don't get paid until Thursday and I've had a shit month, what with my trailer being pinched off the beach and my dog dying... yeah, hm-hm, well, I was thinking something a little bit fancier than Papa Johns, but not as expensive as Domino's... yeah, uh-huh, yes ma'am, and that's why *you're* the boss. Did I tell you I was still chewing the gum you spat at me? Yeah, I know, right, crazy! Completely tasteless, yeah. Uh-huh, well I'll pick you up around eight, yeah? How's that sound? Great, great, great, uh-huh. Okay, see you later, uh-huh. No, *you* hang up. No, YOU hang up! I'm not doing it. Okay *I'll* hang up. Love you, buh-bye. Buh-bye sweetheart. Love you, bye."

Ricks hung up and dropped the phone into his lap.

"All sorted for tonight, then?" Murtow asked, steering around a divot in the road.

Ricks shrugged. "I don't know yet. That was her answer machine. Hopefully, though." He crossed fingers on both hands.

"You really shouldn't be fraternising with the enemy, you know," Murtow said.

"I'm not," Ricks said, apparently shocked by what he was hearing from his partner. "I'm fraternising with the enemy's *accountant*. Big difference, Reg. Biiiiiiig difference."

"Well, I don't think it's very ethical. At least not moral. Like when doctors bang their patients, or when kindergarten teachers bang their—"

"Look, Reg," Ricks interrupted just in the nick of time. "She's in the plot now, and we knew she was gonna have some sort of association to the bad guys, right? It's always the way it goes, otherwise there's no peril later on."

Murtow considered this for a moment in silence. Ricks was right. Breaking the fourth wall, he turned to face the open window and said, "Isn't he always?"

"Did you say something?" Ricks asked, for he was sure his partner had. You never knew with breakers of the fourth wall; sometimes you heard them, others you didn't.

"I didn't say anything," Murtow said. "And anyway, you're going out with Velda Brugenheim tonight?"

"Looks like it," Ricks said. "If she gets my message."

Murtow thought if she did, in fact, get his somewhat unhinged message, Ricks would probably have the night off.

"Well, if anything changes, and I'm starting to think it will—"

"What makes you say that?"

"Let's just say I have a hunch," Murtow said, not to mention a gimpy knee, a watery elbow, a fatty liver, and a warty foreskin. He steered the knackered car around a slow-manoeuvring gaggle of nuns. "Is it a gaggle of nuns? Or a habit? I'm terrible at collective nouns."

"Me too," Ricks said. "I thought it was a *clusterfuck* of nuns. Anyway, you were saying something about a warty foreskin?"

"No I wasn't," said Murtow, and he went back to check his notes. "No, I was just *thinking* about my warty foreskin. I never mentioned it out loud."

"Shall we go back to my last line before all of this got us sidetracked?"

"Nah, I know where we were." He cleared his throat and, like magic or something, he got them both back on track. "And usually, Tish makes dinner for my new partners, and they come round and get to know the family. It's all to make them jealous, really, see what they could have had if they weren't such a monumental fuck-up."

"Shame I'll be busy," Ricks said. "Sounds like a lovely night."

"Yeah, well like I say, if something happens to your new woman, if my hunch is right, the offer still stands."

Thanks," Ricks said. "Sorry about the hunch.

They drove in silence for a while. This little comedown from all the action would inevitably lead to further action before the end of the day. Just then, Murtow's phone rang. He saw that it was Captain Mahone; the little picture of the captain and his wife holidaying somewhere abroad—Paris, Murtow thought, but he didn't know his Eiffel towers from his Blackpool towers, so...—filled the screen as the phone continued to ring. He put it on speaker and said, "Captain?"

When the captain spoke, he sounded frantic, as if the words wouldn't come out quick enough. "Get yourselves to Echo Park!" he said. "I've just had a call from the main bad guy, and he says he' set you two up for something of a puzzle to complete."

Ricks looked at Murtow.

Murtow looked at Ricks.

The conspiracy of cheerleaders Murtow was about to hit dove out of the way, and the passing flamboyance of judges raised their boards and gave the cheerleading group a solid nine out of ten.

Echo Park was suddenly so far away.

Murtow pressed his foot to the floor and the car suddenly lurched forward, as they so often do when you abruptly go from twenty to eighty.

"Finally!" Ricks said, straightening in the passenger seat. "I was beginning to think we were done for the day."

Murtow sulked.

Me too, he thought. *Me too*.

*

The captain hadn't told them where abouts in Echo Park they were to go once they arrived, so they were currently lingering around a hot-dog stand—BUNS IN THE SUN, Est. 1985—awaiting further instructions.

"So, Xavier ain't the main bad guy," Ricks said, from out of nowhere. "This sausage sucks," he also said as he removed the offending brat and tossed it into the beak of a low-swooping pigeon as it passed by.

"What?" Murtow said, nervously pacing this way and that.

"Well, the captain said, 'the main bad guy' when he called," Ricks said, and he said it expecting his partner to understand where he was going. Murtow's angry frown suggested he should explain further. "Up until now we thought Xavier was the main bad guy, and Captain Mahone did, too, since I texted him back in the car—even though it wasn't mentioned in the plot because it wasn't that important—to update him on what we're doing, so why didn't he just say, 'Xavier has a puzzle for you at the park'? He said, 'the main bad guy'. Not Xavier." He tossed his empty wrapper into a nearby trash basket and dusted off his hands.

"I'll be damned!" Murtow said, brightening. "Hey, you really are a good detective."

Ricks was about to say thanks, he already knew that, when Murtow's phone rang. He took it from his pocket, put it on speaker, and then pushed the on-screen answer button.

"Though my grey beginnings are not so pretty, I grow quite well into my beauty. Alabaster white or black as night, my grace is known worldwide. I may make my home in the chilly Arctic, I'm also known well down under. From North America to South, I may be known to trumpet. As a female I may Pen my name, while the males may prefer to pick at a Cob. But near or far my beauty is known by lore and by myth. What am I?"

"On drugs?" Ricks said. Murtow gave him a little kick to the shins.

"I get it," Murtow said. "Your puzzle... it's a *riddle*, and when we solve it, we'll be one step closer to taking you down."

"Ah, Detective Murtow," said the voice. He sounded like a main bad guy, which was probably how he got the job. Not German, Russian, or British, though. Such a shame. "And here I was thinking that new partner of yours was the clever one."

"I am," said Ricks. "I'm good with briefcase combinations and guessing first names. Anything that takes longer than a piss, that's someone else's problem."

"Solve the riddle," said the mysterious voice. "You have five minutes to solve it and get to the next destination. If you are not there by the time I call, well..." He paused there, as if to think. "I mean, I *could* give you an extra few minutes, but only once. I'm a bad guy, not a fucking charity."

"What happens if we don't get there on time?" Murtow said.

"Everyone in the park will die!" said the voice, and then it clicked off.

Ricks looked at Murtow.

Murtow looked at the phone.

The phone screen turned just as blank as the detectives.

"What was the first part again?" Murtow asked. "Something about grey beginnings and Ally Bastard."

"Alabaster," Ricks said. "It means white."

"That makes more sense," Murtow said. "I know Ally Bastard, and he's a lovely fella."

"As a female I may Pen my name," said Ricks, mulling it over.

"While the males may prefer to pick at a Cob," mumbled Murtow.

"Just ask Siri," Ricks said.

"Yeah," said Murtow. "Siri'll know." He fiddled with his phone, fairly fussing over the fingering—

"Just ask the bitch," Ricks said, interrupting the alliteration gag, and not for the last time that day.

And so Murtow did just that, and she *did* know—the clever cunt!— and told him as much.

"Ah!" said Murtow. "All makes sense now, what with a Pen being a female swan and a Cob being a male swan, and alabaster is white, so—"

"The swan boats on Echo Park Lake," Ricks said, and he took off at pace.

Murtow tried to keep up, but he had a hunch, not to mention a gimpy knee and a warty foreskin, and a—

*

"Twelve dollars an hour," said the robbing bastard renting out the boats.

Ricks searched his pockets for the cash, but he knew there was none to be found within. He was just passing time. Twelve dollars an hour! This rogue renter of rickety rafts must have seen them coming. And he had. Ricks's empty hand came out with its middle-finger raised and he shoved it in the general direction of the man.

"Official police business," Murtow said, opening his jacket to reveal his badge, and also the holstered six-shooter.

"Does that thing still even fire?" said the man. "More importantly, how many Victorians has it clocked, huh?" And he laughed, mainly to himself. "What kind of official police business requires a pedalo in the form of a swan, anyway?"

"Probably something fowl," Ricks said, because it was hilarious and punchlines like that might one day make their writer more money than you can shake a tit at.

"Bring her back in one piece," said the man as the detectives climbed aboard. Once seated and suitably buckled in, the man gave them a gentle push with his foot, watched them as they floated farther into the lake, and then moved on to his next customer, who was wheelchair-bound. "Twenty dollars an hour," he said.

*

With a large swan boat, you can glide across the water in style. Perfect for romantic dates or family outings, its large hull for increased buoyancy—

"Knock it the fuck off, Reg!" Ricks said. He would have cuffed his partner about the lug-hole, had he not been strapped in like Hannibal Lector.

The phone rang, the boat rocked, the ducks all flew away, and a wheel-chaired woman capsized nearby.

"That was too easy," Murtow said upon answering the phone.

"Yes, it would appear so," said the voice of the baddie, who was still neither German or Russian, British or Japanese. "Let's see how you get on with my next one. This is a two-parter, so pay attention."

"Bring it on, cocksucker!" Ricks said. He was really starting to enjoy this. Plus with his date tonight—once

Velda got back to him and confirmed it—this could turn out to be his best day on the force ever!

"I go up and I go down but I never move, zat is part eins."

"Did you just slip into a German accent?" Murtow said, confused.

"No!" said the main baddie. "No I didn't!"

"You said zat! You said zat and then you said 'part eins', which means 'part one' I, Ger—"

"Okay, I slipped up," said the voice. "Don't either of you slip up? Huh? I mean, it's just hard being the main bad guy and not being German or Russian, or even British, okay?"

"Sure," Murtow said. "Go ahead and finish your riddle." On the swan beside him, Ricks stifled laughter.

"Part two of the riddle goes like this..." and he cleared his throat. "Ten-times-twenty-plus-eleven-plus-fifty-minus-thirty." The voice fell silent. After a moment it said, "Do you want me to repeat that bit again?"

"No, I've got it," Ricks said. "Pornographic memory, or something," he added.

"You have thirty minutes to solve this problem and get there on time. Failure to do so will result in at least one school in San Marino being closed down permanently. By which I mean blown off the face of the earth. And I know what you're thinking, detectives. That it is past four and that school has already finished for the day. And while you may be correct, do think of those thousands of poor children in after-school clubs and detention. Nothing would give me greater pleasure than to explode those assholes!"

He hung up.

"Sick sonofabitch!" Ricks said, lighting a cigarette and starting to pedal as quickly as he could back toward the rental hut.

"Yeah," Murtow said. "Those poor rich kids going to schools in the San Marino Unified School District." He could not hide his bitterness. He couldn't even afford to send his own seven to Arlington Heights, where the teachers were awful but at least the shootings were up.

"Two-hundred-and-thirty-one," Ricks said, breathlessly, as he pedalled.

"Huh?" Murtow said, half-heartedly pedalling, too. "Two-hundred-and-thirty-one what?"

"That's the answer to my bit of the riddle," Ricks said, huffing out a plume of smoke, which danced away on the LA breeze. Beautiful, it would have been, if lives were not currently at risk. "Your turn. What's something that goes up and goes down but never moves?"

"A yoyo?"

Ricks shook his mullet. "No. Yoyos move if you're walking with them."

"My bank balance?" Murtow was sure he had it this time; it was very true. Anyone with seven kids and a wife will tell you it moves. It moves a fucking lot.

"I'm pretty sure the main bad guy," said Ricks, pausing to catch his breath, "is not aware of your current financial status."

"Stairs!" Murtow snapped.

"Who does?"

"No, stairs. What goes up and down but doesn't move? The answer is stairs."

Ricks thought about this for far longer than he had any right to. They were about to make landfall. The swan rental fella began reversing them into a parking spot. The pedalo swan went *beep, beep, beep*.

"I've got it," Ricks said as they climbed out of the boat. "It's the Baxter Street Stairs. There are two-hundred-and-thirty-one-steps to the Baxter Street Stairs. That's the answer!" He couldn't believe they'd solved another one. And with plenty of time to spare, providing it was still working properly again.

"That's too far away to run," Murtow said, almost slipping on his ass as he disembarked. "He didn't say we had to do it on foot, so we should be able to take the car—"

Just then the phone rang. Murtow answered it.

"I forgot to mention," said the voice of the main baddie. "You must make the journey on foot." And then the voice was gone.

"Fuck," Murtow muttered.

"Fuck indeed," said Ricks.

They began to jog.

"I'm too old for this shit," Murtow said.

Ricks watched him jog and, unfortunately, had to agree. It was like watching an otter try to skateboard.

*

They arrived at the foot of the famous staircase with five minutes to spare. Murtow climbed down off Ricks's back and said thank you and sorry about the pee.

"Let's just hope he doesn't want us to climb up—"

Murtow did eye rollings and answered the phone. Before the bad guy's voice uttered a word, Murtow said, "You want us to go up them, don'tcha?"

"It wouldn't be much of a test now, would it, if I were to make it so simple."

This time Murtow hung up on the baddie. It would have felt pretty good if he didn't feel pretty shit.

The detectives took to the stairs. This time, Ricks made Murtow walk for himself.

Once at the top, and barely able to breathe, let alone speak, they waited for the phone to ring.

"Did we make it in time?" Ricks asked, for he didn't own a watch. Before today, time hadn't been all that important to him. Now it seemed to be all he thought about.

Murtow, on the other hand, owned a number of watches. There was the one he wore on his wrist, the one he wore inside his jacket pocket as if he were a member of the landed gentry, and the one he wore—and *had* worn for five long years—up his ass to give to his dead friend's son when he was old enough to receive it, that was if he didn't die of dysentery first. But now wasn't the time to pull that one out, so he checked the time on his phone.

"Shit, Ricks," he said. "We didn't make it. We're three minutes late.

"Fuck! I told you we shouldn't have stopped for that ice-cream."

"He's gonna blow the school, Ricks."

They both began to panic, and were still panicking when the phone went off one more time.

"You were late," said the bad guy's voice as Murtow answered.

"No, please," Murtow said, thinking of those poor kids in detention or after-school clubs who were about to redecorate the classroom without consent, thinking of his own kids, who thankfully couldn't afford to be in a good school, thinking of how this was going to look when the newspapers and TV stations got a hold of it, all because he was too old for this shit.

"Fortunately for you, detectives, there is no bomb," said the voice. "There never was. I made it all up! What kind of monster do you think I am?"

Ricks looked at Murtow.

Murtow looked at Ricks.

To the phone, Ricks said, "Quite a big one, presently. You've had us running around like headless penises for the last hour, solving your stupid riddles, and for what?" He was fuming. Nay, livid. Nay, incensed! Not to be confused with that thing where you kiss your mom on the naughty bits or marry your sister's brother.

"Shits and giggles," said the main baddie, and hung up.

"I'm going to kill that sonofabitch," Murtow growled.

"Me too," said Ricks. "Shall we call it a day?"

"I think we should," Murtow said as they began to descend the Baxter Street Stairs, all two-hundred-and-thirty-one of the concrete bastards.

*

Up on the forty-fifth floor of Najatomi Heights, there came a roaring of laughter. It had been going on for quite some time. The receptionist, Sandra, sitting in the very next office had become concerned. So perturbed was she that she considered buzzing through to her boss, just to make sure he wasn't trying to tickle himself to death, or something of that nature. She had heard from a friend of a friend, who had read it once in a magazine—the article having been written by someone who had not witnessed it herself, but had been in the same country at the time—that some silly bugger had died watching an old episode of *Friends*. Remarkable, when you think about it; that *Friends* had a joke in it, somewhere. And not only that, but the joke had been so funny it had murdered someone.

Inside the room from which the uncontrollable laughter emanated, Mr. Brandt sat in his chair. It was one of those ones with wheels on it, and he was giving it a jolly good spin as he laughed. His drink was going everywhere.

The bartender, Mac, watched with fascination. He had witnessed the plaguing of the detectives via telephone from behind the bar, and it wasn't all that funny. In fact, Mac thought he had laughed more at an old episode of *Friends* once, and that was positively mirthless.

"Ah, Mac," Brandt said, finally managing to speak. "I can just picture their faces. Had 'em good, didn't we?"

"We, sir?" Mac said. He wanted no part of it.

"Another glass of whisky, my fine man!" said Brandt as he stood and headed toward the window. It wasn't the one he had nudged Sherman Teague through earlier, but one window looks the same in this particular office, so no description is required. "I will be the death of those two," he said, gawping out at the city. His city. A city buzzing with his drugs. "No, really," he said. "I will actually be the death of them; it's already in motion. The wheels they are a-turning, my dearest Mac. Even as we speak, Detective Murtow's home is under surveillance. We'd have the other cop's place covered, too, if it hadn't recently been nicked off the beach."

"Your drink, sir," said Mac, and he was stood right behind Brandt. It made Brandt jump, and not in a nice way.

Brandt took his whisky and returned to his desk. He pushed the buzzer so that he might speak to Sandra. "Sandra, could you cancel my final appointment of the day, please. I'm going to go home early, frantically masturbate, watch a few episodes of *Police Interceptors*, and get my head down for the night. Busy day tomorrow, what with the arrival of my cargo and the meeting with Xavier on the docks to put things right. Have you ever tried my clit, Sandra? It's rather more-ish."

"Can't say I have, Mr. Brandt," Sandra said, her voice coming through the machine like gone-bad treacle.

"Oh, you *can*," Brandt assured her as he lit a huge illegal cigar. It wasn't illegal because it was Cuban. It was illegal because it had recently been used to beat a man to death with. Smoking kills, kiddos! "You can say anything you like to me; it won't go any further."

"I'll cancel your last appointment," Sandra said. "Does that mean I can go home early, as well?"

"Ha! Sandra! Don't start me laughing again. I've only just managed to stop, and I had to think of an old episode of *Friends* to get the job done!"

He took his finger off the intercom.

In the room next to his, and sitting no more than fifty feet away, as the crow flies, a put-upon and much-maligned receptionist muttered, "Cunt."

*

An hour later the office sat empty. Mac the Bartender had gone home, and so too had Sandra, because if Mac could go, then so could she. It was a childish way of thinking, but the way she saw it was this: *Fuck* Mr. Brandt. He wasn't going to fire her, and she was almost sure he wouldn't throw her out the window, as was his wont, because she was a damn fine receptionist, and good receptionists like her—who would also turn a blind eye to the many illegal operations passing across her desk—were hard to come by. So home she had gone, and was currently in the process of peeling potatoes when one of the windows to Mr. Brandt's office exploded inwards. Had she been there to hear it, it would have fairly made her jump, but she wasn't so it didn't.

Glass flew through the air in ultra slow-motion, each shard going over and over and clattering into thing. There was a man in the office now; the man who had come unceremoniously through the window. He landed with a thump on his back, and even though he had been moving in ultra slow-motion, it hurt like a sonofabitch and knocked the wind out of him. He made a, "Herrrrrrrr," sound, which seems to be the default lament when we find ourselves suddenly struggling to breathe. And then, when he finally could, he said, "Fuck, that was stupid."

He climbed slowly to his feet; not ultra slow-motion slowly. By now the budget for that sort of thing has been used up. He untied and removed the firefighter's hose— *utilised in a really expensive scene involving the rooftop of*

Najatomi Heights and a stunt in which a white-vested, barefooted man leapt and dropped twenty feet over the edge of the skyscraper and into the office he now found himself. Yes, it was an awesome scene, but the budget being what it now was, it had been cut out entirely—which had been wrapped thrice around his waist, and was glad to have it off (as most people would be!). In his right hand he gripped a big rusty wrench, which he had managed to purloin from MorkandMindy's broom cupboard when the janitor wasn't looking, for this man was none other than vengeful NYPD dick, Jim McLeod.

Of *course* it was.

"Braaaaaaaandt!" he cried out, in that over-the-top way the hero often does when they're near to the end of the story and the pain of all they have been through is starting to set in.

There was no one but he in the office, as McLeod would have known had he read the first paragraph of this section. Brandt must have gone off to do further bad things, and since his receptionist hadn't come running in to see what the hubbub was all about, McLeod could only assume she'd managed to finagle the rest of the day off. Of Mac the Bartender's existence, McLeod had no idea, so his absence was neither here nor there.

McLeod dusted himself down and pulled bits of bloody glass from his bare feet. And also from his exposed arms. And one thin sliver from his penis. God knows how that got there.

After a slow walk around the room (he didn't mind a few bits of glass in his feet, but there was no need to be silly about it) he arrived at the bar. It was, he noticed, a very well-kept bar, with plenty of choice. McLeod chose the *Um Bongo!* because he never drank on the job.

He now found himself at Brandt's desk, staring down at a picture frame. It wasn't because he had a hard-on for home decor—this particular frame wasn't even that nice—but because he recognised the woman in the photograph contained within. McLeod's ex-wife, Molly. Molly McLeod, she had once been, but the last he heard, she had reverted to her maiden name, Generic.

"Molly motherfucking Generic," McLeod muttered. He had no idea of the alliteration running gag going on in other areas of the plot, so there was no cause for celebration. It had been a simple fluke.

He gently placed the photo face-down on the desk. He couldn't look at it any longer. His ex-wife was fuck-ugly, and he'd always thought so. It's only after you're rid of someone for good that you can finally admit it to yourself and think it out loud.

No longer terrorised by the picture of his ex-wife—who had a face like a burst sofa—McLeod pulled open and riffled through the desk drawers, unsurprised to find that the bottom one was for junk only. There were band-aids and old phones and paperclips and those little birthday candles and—

"Stick to the plan, McLeod," he urged himself, slamming the junk drawer shut. It is a known fact that the three most difficult habits to kick in the US are drinking, taking drugs, and going through someone else's junk drawer when they're not in the room.

McLeod had saved himself just in the nick of time.

He turned on Brandt's computer—his printer was also fairly aroused, but because it was currently out-of-order, it didn't spew white paper across the office, the way it might have done—and a screen appeared, requesting a four-digit password.

"One-two-three-four," McLeod said, pushing the keys as he spoke. When that didn't work he keyed in *five-six-seven-eight*, and was soon able to access all manner of accounts and important classified documents, as well as *Minecraft*.

"I'll be fucking damned," McLeod said, for it seemed Brandt had his fingers in *all* the pies, not just McLeod's ex-wife.

Extortion, prostitution, trafficking, narcotics distribution, tax evasion, Brandt was into all of it, but there was one file-folder missing on Brandt's desktop, and so McLeod created it there and then.

DOG KILLING.

He added one file to the folder, simply entitled: Wicksy, for that had been McLeod's poor boy's name. The name of the dog Brandt had tossed into the canal.

McLeod had a good cry about it for a few minutes, then got back to work.

On top of the desk was a post-it note with some scribblings upon it. "How did you miss this, Jim?" he said, peeling the luminous yellow post-it from the desk. He looked at it.

It looked back at him, somehow.

"The docks, midnight tomorrow" McLeod said, reading front the note. "Huge shipment of *clit*." He had never heard of it, but it sounded like something that would be impossible to find if you didn't already know where it was.

And now McLeod knew where it would be tomorrow night, and also where to find and finish Brandt, once and for all.

"The docks it is," said he, and then he laughed, for it was far funnier than an old episode of *Friends*.

McLeod could have left via the shattered window, but he took the elevator down instead. He had clocked off for the evening.

Just as everyone else involved seemingly had.

11

Ricks was in his hotel room, working his way through the mini-bar and an old episode of *Friends* when she called. He'd all but given up on Velda Brugenheim, and had had a good mind to spit out the chewing gum she had given him earlier that day as a token of her love, but here she was, calling him back—of course she was! Women couldn't get enough of the mullet and almost-Australian accent—and saying, "I've booked us a table at Dino's Famous Chicken, I hope you don't mind."

Well, Ricks *did* mind, actually. He'd had his heart and mind set on pizza all day. Was this how things were going to be with Velda? Her holding all the power and taking control of things like choosing chicken over a thick-crust twelve-inch (that's what she said) Meat Feast? That had been one of the things he'd enjoyed about being a widow; not having to consult another person about where to eat. Another thing was leaving the toilet seat up. He absolutely *loved* that. Couldn't get enough of it. Sometimes he pissed all over the place on purpose, playing penis pirouette, prancing practically—

"Are you still there?" Velda asked. "Have I annoyed you by making the arrangements for our date?"

"No!" Ricks said, through gritted teeth. They were teeth that could be used in toothpaste advertisements. Teeth that were printed on canvases and distributed to dentists across the land. They were good teeth, in other words. Pity she couldn't see them down the phone. "It's just that... well, my dead wife, Becky, she always used to let me sort out our date nights." He tried not to sound too disappointed; he was, after all, hoping to have some intercourse at the end of it, and no one liked a whiner.

"Oh, Ricks, I am sorry!" she said. "I didn't know you had a dead wife. How remiss of me!"

"That's okay," Ricks said. "She's been dead for almost two weeks now. It's time to move on, and I can't expect you to be anything like her, Velda. I would hate it if you *were*."

"Why? Because it would hurt to be reminded of her?

"No," Ricks said. "Because she wasn't very nice."

There was a brief pause, a moment of deafening silence, then: "So we are good for the chicken place?" Velda said. Ricks could hear her smile, if such a thing were possible.

"Chicken is fine by me," said Ricks. "I'd pick you up, but someone recently set fire to my car."

"*Christ*, Ricks!" she said. "You are having terrible luck at the moment. First your dead wife, then your trailer being stolen, and now your car being set alight."

"No wonder I think about swallowing a bullet every night," he said, picking his Beretta up from the duvet and admiring it as if *it* was the one going out on a date with him, and not Velda.

"What?"

"What? I didn't say *anything* about being suicidal." *Phew*, he thought. *Got away with that one*. Women *never* find clinically- and majorly-depressed men attractive, no matter *how* much they pretend to. Becky had tolerated his propensity to do terrible things to himself, but never once had she asked to join in.

And ultimately, after his many years of trying to end *himself*, it had been *her* to go first.

Ricks wished he'd never brought her that stupid trampoline now, God rest her soul.

"I'll just have a quick shit, shower, shave," Ricks said. "And I'll meet you there."

He hung up. Shit, showered, shaved. Met her there.

"Wow!" he said as she climbed out of the cab. "That was quick. You look amazing, Velda."

And she did. Her stunning black dress, short enough to reveal to Ricks what might be in store later on, but not short enough to have her arrested before so much as a chicken nugget touched her lips.

Her lips were beautiful, painted slightly red and glossed to perfection, and Ricks could imagine what it would be like to kiss her, and he liked what he imagined. He would have to wait, though—as they weren't at that stage yet—and settled for a simple fist-bump as she stepped up onto the kerb and smiled.

It was a gorgeous smile, and those dimples, the cutest of divots in her face that looked deep enough to house a thousand refugees or all of the Kardashians, made an appearance. Ricks had a semi-on, and thought that the sooner they were seated within, the better.

Dino's Famous Chicken was not a restaurant at all. It was a bog-standard chicken shop with all of the presumed fixtures and fittings of such an establishment. There were six tables, flanked on both sides by low benches, the whole ensemble affixed permanently to the dirty tiles beneath, because you never quite know when someone might suddenly need a plastic table-and-chairs and decide to run off with them after their meal.

Behind the high counter—so high that only the tops of people's heads could be seen going this way and that—and taking up most of the wall was a menu lit by lights (what else? Candles?) and a kebab that hadn't been a kebab for years rotated slowly upon a vertical spit, at the rear of which were the things keeping it lukewarm so patrons didn't die immediately; at least allowing them to get home first before their stomachs emptied and their assholes exploded all over the—

"Table for two?"

Ricks pulled his gun out and pointed it at the Middle Eastern man who had appeared out of thin air. The man flung his arms into the air and his eyelids to the ceiling, for he was shocked, and make no mistake about it.

"No, Ricks!" Velda said, gently pushing his arm down so that the gun was lowered. "He's our server."

Ricks was unsure whether to trust this—he glanced down at the plastic nametag affixed to the man's breast—Faiz. He had been in situations not dissimilar to this (nothing like this, actually) and had lost buddies because of his mistakes. How many brothers had he lost because of his actions or inactions? *Never again*, he thought. He raised the gun once more, squeezing the trigger ever-so-slightly. Just another pound of pressure and the gun would fire.

Velda lowered it once more. "Behave yourself, Ricks," she said, offering Faiz a smile that said, *I'm ever-so-sorry. I can't take him anywhere, but be assured I will punish him later. I will punish him real good*. She licked her painted lips. Faiz looked away, for this was starting to get weird.

Ricks shoved his Beretta away from whence it came, offered something resembling an apology to their server, Faiz, and allowed himself to be led three feet across the room to a table yet to be cleared up and wiped down.

"Will this be okay?" Faiz said, gathering up boxes filled with half-devoured chicken drumsticks and then dusting the salt desert someone had left onto the floor.

"This will be fine," Velda said, glancing about the place. "Lovely," she added. "Just lovely."

"The menu, as you can see, is behind the counter on the wall, lit up by lights, definitely not candles. When you are ready to order, just shout it somewhere in the direction of the kitchen, which is not a kitchen at all, really. More of a cell with a cooker and a mountain of boxes with our logo printed on them reaching from floor to ceiling. Your chicken will be delivered to you lukewarm in just a few seconds. Would you like to see the drinks menu?"

Ricks nodded. "That would be—"

"It's Coke or Pepsi!" Faiz interrupted rather loudly. "That is the menu. The whole drinks menu. At a stretch we can make it diet, but that means we have to get Hakim to suck out all the sugar using a straw, and that takes time, so..." He shrugged, as if to say, *Just have regular Coke or Pepsi, it's not worth the hassle.*

"We'll just have a family bucket, four regular fries, two cokes—give Hakim the night off—and all the dips you've got, apart from that green one with the bits floating about on top."

Faiz smiled, did a little curtsey, and went off (*went off a long time ago*, Ricks thought, blowing his nose on a napkin he'd picked up from the floor.)

"Nice here, isn't it?" Velda said, and without any irony, too. Amazing how she kept a straight face.

"Yeah," Ricks replied. "Why did you choose this place in particular?"

"Oh, it's only down the road from where I live," she said.

"But you came in a taxi," Ricks frowned. They didn't say he was a great detective for nothing. Sometimes they were bribed.

"I don't get out much," Velda said. "Wanted to make a night of it. No expense spared, that sort of thing."

Ricks nodded. He knew exactly what she meant.

The food arrived then, and it was just as expected. Inedible pieces of chicken, from which it was impossible to identify the body part; Ricks pulled a long, thin, crispy-coated tail from the bucket and set it down on the table. You didn't have to be a great detective to know this particular piece of chicken came from a rat. He would stick to the fries.

As Faiz lit tall candles and set them down around the unpacked meal, he sang. It was all a bit ridiculous, Ricks thought, but Velda seemed to be enjoying herself. She wasn't even questioning the food. Probably because it might have answered back.

Over in the corner, and yet not ten feet away, the nailed-down bench had been removed to make way for a strange half-woman (nothing from the waist down, which was the best way to be if you were a half-person) who sat upright on a hospital bed with a basket of kebab in her lap. Two what appeared to be nurses fussed over her—changing drips, cleaning lines, and swapping out catheters, which made absolutely no sense as there was nothing to stick the catheter into, not anymore. The girl pushed dry kebab into her face and yelled into a phone, which was attached to the bedframe and was recording the woman as she ate. "Don't forget to like and subscribe," the woman said around a mouthful of chewed mystery meat. "Seven out of ten, guys. Seven out of ten." Some food fell out of her mouth and landed on the back of the second nurse's head as she unloaded a catheter bag into a nearby mop bucket. "Dino's Famous Chicken, seven out of ten, that's a review." And then the woman went back to sleep and the nurses, now finished with their duties, wheeled the hospital bed out of the building, shouting thanks across their shoulder to Faiz and Hakim and Dino as they went.

"Oh my God!" Velda said, somewhat excitedly. "That was BoujeeQueen27. I can't believe it, Ricks!"

Ricks, who had watched the entire thing wishing he was dead, shrugged. "What the hell is a boujee queen twenty-seven?"

"Only the most famous TokTiker of all," said she. "She got caught up in that car chase this morning, the one all over the news, and was cut in half by the getaway car."

"Shame," Ricks said, dipping a cold fry in garlic mayo and tossing it over his shoulder. It was easier that way; cut out the middleman. He was done eating. Dino's Famous Chicken was a great way to lose weight. "Didn't think they would have been able to save her, with injuries like that."

"They can do anything these days," said his future-wife. "She'll be up and about in no time."

"Fannyless," Ricks said, trying to imagine what that might look like. Would everything just come to a stop, or would there be some sort of tapering? As if she'd been put through a pencil sharpener. Some questions needed to be asked; this one, Ricks thought, should never be asked out loud.

There was ambient music on now and the lights were dimmed just for the couple at table six. The candles flickered, the cokes arrived, and were the only warm things on the table. A Rasta on crutches came in, begged Faiz for a drumstick, promised he wouldn't return for the rest of the night if he were to just, "Help a brother out!"

"Every night with you, Trevor," Faiz said, passing a napkin-wrapped piece of chicken across the counter. "Where's your boom-box tonight?"

"Don't ask," the Rasta said, before bidding the restaurant-that-wasn't-a-restaurant-at-all a good evening and limping out, his napkin-wrapped chicken stuffed into his armpit as he went.

"I'm really enjoying myself tonight, Ricks," said Velda, dabbing at her lips with a napkin that was almost certainly the one Ricks had blown his nose into a moment ago.

"Me too," Ricks lied. Present company excluded, he had hated every moment of it so far, and yearned for his hotel room, where there was air-con and a mini-fridge and definitely no half-people milling about the place or—

"How did she die?" Velda said, slurping at her coke through a paper straw that was already on its last legs. "Your wife, how did she pass?"

"It was a freak trampoline accident," Ricks said. God, it hurt to think about. "Neither of us knew it was for outdoor use only. There was nothing on the box—"

"It's okay, Ricks," Velda said, reaching across the table, where she took his hand into her own. "If it's too soon to, well, you know, if all this is too soon for you—"

"It's been a fortnight already," Ricks said sadly. "And she always said to me, did Becky, she always said to me, *if I die before you, I want you to go out and find someone else. Don't mourn for me, Ricks. Get that dick of yours good and wet.* This is what she wanted for me." He wiped a tear that had accumulated at the corner of his eye.

Velda nodded. "Sounds like a wonderful woman," she said.

"She was," Ricks said, trying to think of one other example of *how* she was. Like the OceanGate submersible, he came up empty.

Faiz arrived presently at the table. He was playing a violin now and had a rose clenched between his teeth. Velda smiled as she watched him perform, and Ricks watched Velda, gazed into those wonderfully deep dimples of hers and thought, *I bet she has to use a toothbrush to get them all clean inside.*

Why would someone so beautiful, so wonderfully his cup-of-tea, work for someone as rakish as Percival Xavier? He would ask her, but not tonight. Tonight was all about her. It was also about fulfilling Becky's dying wish, of course, but mainly it was about making Velda happy.

He moved the chewing gum from one cheek to the other. It was as hard as a rat's bollock, now. *Might even be one*, Ricks thought as he stared into the half-finished family bucket.

"Would you walk me home?"

Ricks looked up to find Faiz and his violin gone and Velda Brugenheim counting change out onto the salt-and-dip coated table. Was he going to allow her to pay? Of course not! He took out his wallet, removed a bill, and smooshed it into a blob of mayo on the table.

"Of course," Ricks said, blowing out the candles. "In fact," he also said, taking out his phone and punching a number into the screen, "why not push the boat out?"

An automated voice—not unlike Stephen Hawking sitting on the shitter—informed them that their cab would arrive in less than fifteen minutes.

*

Velda's apartment was so close to the chicken shop that the cab driver refused payment. In fact, he gave *them* five dollars and, having noticed the restaurant pick-up point, thanked them for not throwing up all over his back seat.

"Well, I've had a lovely time, Ricks," Velda said as they stood on the steps leading up to her front door. Buzzers surrounded the door, each one connected to the corresponding apartment number. It was all Ricks could do not to buzz them all and make a run for it. Maybe another, less romantic time

"It's been nice," Ricks agreed, though quite why that half-woman had rated it seven-out-of-ten was beyond him.

Velda leaned in, and so did Ricks, and their lips met in the middle, which came as a surprise to no one, least of all the kissers. When they were done, they separated. Ricks sighed and smiled, Velda smiled and sighed, and they both stood, speechless in the moment, although Ricks's semi-on was further taking to the vertical plane.

"I would invite you in," Velda said, "but I have the painters and decorators in, so—"

"Oh!" Ricks said. "Don't worry about that. A bit of blood doesn't bother me. I was in Iraq."

Just then, the door to Velda's building opened and two workmen, complete with paint-stained overalls and carrying a ladder, came through it. "Not quite finished I'm afraid, Ms. Brugenheim," said the burly one at the front.

"Should be done by tomorrow, though," added the one at the rear." Noticing Ricks, he said, "Oh, Barry! This poor fucker thought he was going to get some tonight."

Barry, the one at the front of the ladder, gave Ricks a once-over. "That's horrible," he said. "Listen, I've had blue balls before, and it ain't pleasant, but you'll get over it, dude."

Ricks took out his Beretta and the workmen quickly fell silent. Funny how that worked, wasn't it? They continued to load their truck in silence.

"Sorry again," said Velda. "The fumes must be terrible up there, and there's no point both of us being unconscious—"

"I completely understand," Ricks said. "I'd ask you back to my hotel room, but they're ever-so-fussy about extra guests."

Velda giggled cutely.

Ricks laughed frustratedly.

The workmen watched silently.

"I'd love to do this again," Velda finally said. It was getting cold now and she was starting to feel it; Ricks could see it in her nipples, which also told him it was presently quarter-past-eleven.

"I love you," he said.

"What?"

"*What*? I said I can't *wait*."

"I have two tickets to a concert on Thursday night," she said brightly, as if she had only just remembered, and she had. "Won them in a competition at work. I wasn't going to go alone, but *now*—"

"I'd love to!" Ricks said, for Thursday was not too far away and blue-balls were only temporary. "Who is playing?"

"Yoko Ono," she said.

"I can't do Thursday," Ricks said, "but I'll definitely call you tomorrow."

They said their goodbyes, kissed a little more, and Ricks watched as she made her way up the steps to her building, where she let herself in, but not before turning to give one final parting gift to Ricks. She blew him a kiss. And although he would have preferred a fresh piece of gum, it was still all very nice. And then she was gone, saved for a future date, off to her bed alone for now.

His beautiful Velda.

His future-wife.

Becky Ricks, God rest her soul, would have been proud.

Ricks wanked a lot that night, giving his own room, albeit temporary, a fresh coat of off-white.

12

When Ricks awoke the next morning, it wasn't calm and unhurried, as he usually liked it. He was unceremoniously pulled from his dream—a chaste affair with Velda, in which both of them were virgins and neither of them knew what went where and how long it stayed there for—by the ringing of the telephone on the bedside table. Who could have been calling him in his temporary hotel room? At this time in the morning? And why? These were all questions simply answered when he took up the handset and said, "What the flying fuck—"

A frantic voice interrupted and overpowered his own, and he listened as the owner of the voice, Captain Mahone of the LAPD and his new boss, told him to get over to Murtow's place post-haste, for there was chaos currently unwrapping and underway and Murtow's life depended on it.

"I'm on my way," Ricks said, already pulling himself into his too-tight jeans and running an alcohol-withdrawn shaky hand through his mullet.

What had they gotten themselves into?

Ricks arrived on scene a little over an hour later. Public transport wasn't what it used to be, and he cursed the sonofabitch who had recently torched his car.

Upon his arrival, the little officer with the wonky eyes from the station yesterday stopped cordoning the street off and rushed across several lawns to get to him.

"Detective Rickth, ain't it?" the cop said, "Murtow'th thuithidal and unhinged new partner?"

Ricks didn't stop walking, and the little fella was having a helluva time keeping up. "Do you kiss your mother with that mouth?" he asked.

"Um, my mother'th dead," said the rookie, and now his eyes weren't just going one way or the other; they were rolling each and every way like a confused magic eight ball.

Did Ricks feel bad for the kid? No. Should he have brought mothers into it so soon? Probably not.

Just then the bomb squad pulled up, and several men jumped out of the vehicle, all decked out in EOD suits. One of the men took out a little robot thingamajig and, using a remote control, steered it along the sidewalk toward the Murtow residence. It was all very thrilling, but Ricks was not interested in what was going on around him.

Murtow needed him.

"Do you think he'll be okay?" the wonky-eyed rookie said. He was running alongside Ricks now, breathlessly enunciating and punctuating each word.

"Gee, kid, I don't even know what's happening!" Ricks said, finally snapping. "And what is your name, anyway? I'm sick of this narrator sonofabitch using your wonky eyes as a descriptor. It's really bad form."

"It's Bothi, thir," he said. "Offither Bothi."

Boss-eye.

Ricks had had enough. The wordplay was getting out of control.

Leaving Bossi in the capable hands of Kowalski, who was making the most of the coconut shy that had been erected on the lawn in front of Murtow's next-door neighbours' house, Ricks headed inside, where it was even more chaotic than outside.

There must have been twenty cops in total milling about downstairs in the foyer and its adjacent rooms, ten more helping themselves to the food in the Murtow family's refrigerator. A few more were stood about smoking in the backyard. SWAT—whatever *they* were doing here, as shooting a bomb was often the worst way to defuse it, although it did speed things up a little—had raided the shed and were now starting a swing-ball tournament next to the Koi pond. The entire department, it seemed, had come to see Reginald P. Murtow explode, and Ricks wondered just how crazy *he* was, after all, when these idiots were all just... stood about, waiting for a bomb in their vicinity to do its thing.

He made his way up the stairs; the sign sellotaped to the wall which read BOMB AND TERRIFIED DETECTIVE THIS WAY ↖ was unnecessary, Ricks thought, but under other circumstance, ones which didn't involve the life of his partner—not to mention his own—he might have been the one to print the sign out. Hell, he'd have coloured it in and splashed a bit of glitter over it. Really, whoever had made this sign had done a piss-poor job.

Amateurs.

At the top of the stairs stood Captain Mahone. When he saw Ricks, he gave his ice-cream one last lick and handed it to a uniformed cop, who took it away for disposal.

"Glad you could make it," the captain said, sarcastically.

"Fucking bus," Ricks said. "I was waiting for half-an-hour, then twelve came at once."

"Like a bukkake," said Mahone, nodding thoughtfully.

"What?"

"Never mind. Look, Ricks, he's in a pretty bad way in there, so I want you to calm him down, yeah?"

Ricks suddenly felt like he was the last person for this particular job. "I'll do my best, captain," he said, "but I have to tell you, I'm probably the last person for this particular job."

"Just keep him talking for five minutes, just until we can get the bomb squad in there to take care of it so we can all get on with our day."

Ricks nodded. "What are the chances of getting him out of there alive?" It was a question he hadn't wanted to ask, and the answer that came terrified him.

"Boo!" said Mahone.

That's quite enough of that, Ricks thought, and moved past the captain, reached the bathroom door, took a deep breath, and went in.

The bathroom smelt of shit. Of course it did; it was a bathroom, and it was currently in use. The thing was, had Murtow shit before he discovered the bomb, or had he found it and then, as a natural response, done some serious shitting? Either way, Ricks had to fight the dizziness to stay on his feet. When Murtow saw him, he brightened a little. Ricks wanted to tell him not to get his hopes up, that he shouldn't pin his likelihood of survival on a man who chewed the end of his pistol every night before bed. Ricks entertained death, courted and welcomed it even, daily. His arrival should have been the last thing Murtow wanted. Yet there he sat, smiling and full of hope.

Another nugget fell from his arse and plopped into the water below.

"Hey, Reg," Ricks said, suddenly aware of how strange the situation was. "Got yourself in a bit of a pickle, by the looks of it."

Murtow nodded; a bead of sweat dripped from the tip of his nose and landed on his exposed aubergine. "Could say that, Ricks," he said, almost a whisper, his nervous smile fading.

Outside the cramped bathroom, somebody started to clear the hallway. "Dead man sitting!" said a voice. It was Kowalski—that inconsiderate sonofabitch—and he sounded almost gleeful as he ushered officers out of upstairs rooms. "Everybody downstairs and out of the house, we've got a dead man sitting. Hey, where did you find that? Murtow's wife's knickers drawer? Put it back. She's probably gonna need it even more after today."

"I'll kill him," Murtow said.

"You won't have to," Ricks said. And then, for no other reason than to change the subject, he added, "Hey! Remember that time we were on that swan pedalo?" He seated himself on the edge of the bathtub opposite his partner.

Murtow smiled as if in fond remembrance. "Yeah," he said. "And you were about to put a bullet in the guy that rented them out." He shook his head and smiled even wider. "Echo Park Lake... man, feels as though it was just yesterday

"Yeah," Ricks said. "Because it was."

"It sure was."

"Hm."

There came an awkward silence, which Ricks wanted to fill, so he did.

138

"How the hell did this happen?" he asked. Like, 'If one synchronised swimmer drowns, do the others have to drown, too?' it was a damn good question.

"Tish had to go to work early," Murtow sighed. Ricks could tell this was going to be a long story, so he made himself comfortable. At least, as comfortable as you could possibly get perched on the edge of a bathtub. "So, she dropped the kids off at school. They have this breakfast club, you know? It's mainly for bad parents who can't be bothered to make their kid's breakfast, but we use it from time to time, when Tish has to go in early, or we've run out of Froot Loops."

"Uh-huh," Ricks said. This monologue was Murtow's yes, but that didn't mean he wouldn't pop up every now and then, if only to remind the reader he was still there.

"I had the house to *myself*, Ricks, and I realised, I hadn't had the house to myself for *months*. Shit, usually I can't even have the bathroom to myself. Five fucking kids, Ricks—"

"Seven," Ricks mumbled.

"*Seven* fucking kids, Ricks! You know what they say about rats in New York, about you never being more than six feet away from a rat at any given time?"

Ricks nodded. He had heard *something* like that, but it might have been: in Hollywood, you're never more than six feet away from a Skarsgård. It amounted to the same thing.

"That's what it's like when you've got seven fucking kids, Ricks."

"Does Tish know you liken your offspring to rodents?" Ricks said as he fiddled with a bar of soap. When he saw the black pube deeply embedded in it, he set it back down.

"This morning, though, I had peace. I had peace and I had the place to myself, if only for a half-an-hour. So, I decided to make the most of it. I came up here with my magazine—" he gestured to the magazine between his feet: *Cockhandlers Today - Issue 109*, "—and a glass of Buck's Fizz, got myself settled in, and that was when..." He trailed off there. Ricks would have to finish the sentence for him.

"That was when you realised you should have worn more condom in life," he said.

"No!" Murtow said. Ricks made a mental note that they had to work on finishing each other's sentences. "That was when I dropped my phone," Murtow said. "See, you might think you have the place to yourself, but really, you don't. You have to take your phone *everywhere* with you, just in *case*. In *case* Tish needs to remind me to take out the trash; in *case* one of the kids has an accident at breakfast club; in case, in case, in case—"

"So you dropped your phone," Ricks said, urging his partner to get back on track.

"Yeah!" Murtow said. "And when I reached for it... that was when I felt it, Ricks."

"The bomb?"

"The bomb," Murtow said, and he visibly shuddered. He also noisily farted as something or other fell out of him, and then physically winced as toilet water jumped up to splash his ass. "I knew it was a bomb when I felt the wire. Then it made this godawful buzzing noise, Ricks, and I thought I was a dead man right there and then. Dead man sitting, just like Kowalski said."

Ricks pinched the bridge of his nose between thumb and forefinger.

"Hey!" Murtow said, batting Ricks's hand away. "Pinch your own damn nose!"

"Okay, enough of this," Ricks said. He jumped up from the edge of the bathtub and dropped down onto his knees. "Let's get you out of here before people start talking about us."

"Hey, Ricks, maybe wait for the bomb squad, yeah?"

"Sure!" Ricks said, shuffling his way past Murtow's tremulous legs. "In the meantime, this bomb could go off anyway and take me with it." He managed to squeeze himself into the space between Murtow's left thigh and the wall. It was quite a snug fit. Most LA realtors would have said the space was a *cosy* one, with potential as a second bedroom.

"Go!" Murtow yelled at his partner. "There's no point us both dying in here, Ricks! You're young, I'm too old for this shit, and—"

"No one is dying in here," Ricks said.

"How can you be so sure?" Murtow was frantic now. It was as if all of this—his monologue, Kowalski sending people away, him comparing his kids to vermin, Ricks finding the black pube in the soap, the *Cockhandler* magazine, the bomb squad currently making their way upstairs, all of it—had been leading up to this moment. And it was all going to come to a head when Ricks said:

"It's fucking *Operation*, Reg!"

Murtow opened his eyes. He hadn't even realised he'd shut them. "Huh?"

Ricks backed out of the area next to the toilet (*good for storage, perfect for bunkbeds*) and in his hand was that veritable sonofabitch of a game, *Operation*. The naked patient with the LED light for a nose seemed to grin at them both. His innards were completely empty, though, as nothing could be heard rattling around inside, and Ricks gave it a jolly good shake to make sure.

"It was *Operation*!" Murtow said. He looked as if he might lose his mind, or already had. "I felt the wire, and then, then, the buzzing, and it was, it was just *Operation*!"

"One of your kids must have been playing with it in here," Ricks said, though who plays a game that tests a player's hand-eye coordination, as well as fine motor skills, whilst taking a shit was beyond him.

"Hey, Ricks!" Murtow said as he wiped himself and grinned. He stood from the toilet, using the wall to steady himself. "It was just *Operation*. It was just *Operation*, Ricks!"

"Yeah, but we've got a problem," Ricks said, realising that they had a problem.

The crazed grin fell from Murtow's face and landed somewhere between them. "Oh," he said. He quickly pulled his pants up; Ricks was glad to see the back of that thing, whatever it was. "You mean, the problem is that it's just *Operation*?"

Ricks nodded.

"And that the whole department is outside, including the bomb squad—"

"And SWAT," Ricks said.

"What the fuck are SWAT doing here. Don't they know that shooting a bomb is not the best way to defuse it?"

"Speeds things up a bit," Ricks said.

"Shit, Ricks, I'm gonna be the laughing stock of the whole department. They're gonna be leaving board games everywhere. On my desk, *Monopoly*, in my drawers, *Boggle*; fuck, Ricks, I'm never gonna hear the end of this."

He was right. His mistaking a vintage board-game for an actual explosive device—an error absolutely anyone could make, provided that they were an actual idiot in the first place—would not go down well with the captain.

"I've got an idea," Ricks said. Whether it would work remained to be seen, but he couldn't just stand by and let Murtow take a hit. He couldn't take it the way Ricks could. Didn't have the sense of humour to get over it. "Hand me that towel."

"Wait, what are you going to do?" asked Murtow, for he was genuinely intrigued, and also slightly concerned that whatever Ricks was about to do would make things even worse. He handed Ricks the towel anyway.

"On three," Ricks said, wrapping *Operation* up in the towel.

"Your three or mine?" Murtow asked, unsure what was going to happen on three, *whoever* the three belonged to.

"One," Ricks said.

"Two."

"Th—"

*

The bathroom door exploded outwards, knocking an unfortunately-positioned bomb-disposal fella, and his little robot, too, out of the way. *"Everybody out of the way!"* Ricks bellowed. Beneath his armpit, wrapped in a bath-towel, was what everyone watching took to be the bomb. Murtow was right behind him. Quite why he was running along with the bomb and its carrier was a mystery to everyone, or would have been had they really sat down and had a good think about it.

"Out of the way!" Murtow cried as both he and Ricks took the stairs two, even three at a time. Admittedly, Ricks was doing it on purpose; Murtow was simply falling behind his partner, and would have fallen completely had Ricks not been in front of him. *"It's gonna blow!"*

"Yeah!" Ricks yelled. *"Everyone outtatheway! It's definitely a bomb and it's definitely gonna blow!"*

Out into the early morning sunlight they raced, raising Hell and screaming bloody murder as they reached Murtow's battered car and hastened into it.

Sirens and flashing lights went on as the car peeled out of the driveway and laid down some rubber on the street. Hundreds of cops watched them go, some applauding while others made the sign of the cross.

"True American heroes," Captain Mahone said, lighting his thirtieth cigarette of the day.

In the car that had left the street, the one that could no longer be seen by those surrounding Murtow's house, the one with one door completely off and a spiderwebbed windshield—Ricks tossed the towel-covered *Operation* board-game, which was definitely not a bomb about to go off, into the back seat and looked at Murtow.

Murtow looked at Ricks.

And together, with a mixture of disbelief and sudden relief, they laughed so hard Ricks almost lost his gum.

13

Stacked floor to ceiling with black-and-white screens, each displaying a different office, board room, storage cupboard, shower cubicle—just in case someone decided to steal the soap, of course—the CCTV room at Najatomi Heights made whirrings and chirpings and clickings as it went about its business. Its business was to capture moments of criminality, and it did a damn good job of it, so long as there wasn't a city-wide power-cut or the satellite providing the building with wi-fi didn't suddenly nip behind a cloud.

The man responsible for the building's security—a young Japanese fella by the name of Endo, who you would immediately recognise if you were to encounter him on the street, because he had been in loads of things, but if the subject of his name came up, you'd simply shrug and say, "Never 'eard of 'im."—was spinning in his spinny chair when there came a knock at the door.

Being Head of Security, and also Chief CCTV Operator (Grade 3 Diploma), Endo had at his disposal all the latest technology, and yet not one camera, and there were literally thousands of them in Najatomi Heights, pointed down at the door to his security hub.

It was, as they say in the trade—*what trade? Most trades*—a fucking joke.

Endo kicked at his desk, which took him spinning across the room on his chair, which was not just a spinny one, but also it was on wheels. He came to a stop in front of the door, which knocked again, this time more urgently.

"Better not be 'monitoring' the shower cubicles' again in there." It was Mr. Brandt, the only man Endo knew who could use single quotation marks in a sentence and make them heard.

Endo stood, entered the four-digit-code on the pad next to the door (which was, of course, *one-two-three-four*) and sat again. By the time the door had fully whispered open, he was back at his desk, perusing the infinite screens before him.

"What is it I can do for you, sir?" Endo asked, not taking his eyes from the multitude of monitors manned mainly by men, monotonous might—

"Don't start all that nonsense while I'm trying to speak," said Brandt to no one in particular. "Endo, I need you to check something for me. My office, at some point overnight, appears to have had a visitor." He had a damn good idea who it might be: either Ricks, Murtow, or both of them, the desecration of his workspace a retaliation for making a mockery of them yesterday.

"A *visitor*, Mr. Brandt?" Endo was doing magical things with his hands and fingers—which is why he had been happily married for going on ten years, now—and so quickly that they were all a-blur. Brandt was momentarily mesmerised, and this time the alliteration was necessary.

"Yes, a *visitor*, Endo," Brandt said, giving up on watching the Japanese man's invisible hands and turning his attention back to the screens taking up the majority of the wall in front.

"Any idea what time this visitor stopped by?" Endo asked, for no other reason than it made his job a lot easier,

"And how might I know that, Endo?" Brandt said, growing tired of silly questions already, and it was only half-past-eight.

"Perhaps they left a note, sir," Endo said. "A little letter saying 'Stopped by at eleven, but you weren't here. All the best, Darren. xx'. That sort of thing."

"They didn't leave a note, Endo, and—who the bloody hell is Darren, and why's he leaving kisses on the end of his notes to me?"

"How should I know, sir," Endo said. "He's *your* secret nocturnal visitor."

"He is not!" Brandt said. "Never met the man in my life."

Endo decided not to press Mr. Brandt further. What went on in the confines of his own office was his business. Unless Endo happened to be watching the Brandt Enterprises cameras at the time, as he now was, then it was his business, too. It was all very confusing, and Endo decided to stop thinking about it before the hamster wheel in his head came off its arms.

The captured video of Mr. Brandt's office now came up on all the screens at once, not as a thousand little offices but as one large one. It was amazing what you could do with technology these days, and Brandt said as much with his singular, "Wow!" And then, noticing how grainy the picture was, he added, "Oh."

The video footage moved rapidly in reverse for several seconds, and then they saw it, sort of. A bald man wearing a dirty white vest was putting things back in drawers, then handing something in at the bar, before falling to the ground and then throwing himself backwards and out the window, which he fixed before he left. It was remarkable to behold, even better in reverse than it had been going forward.

"Now play it forward," Brandt said, seating himself on the edge of the desk and staring raptly up at the huge display.

Endo pushed play and leaned back in his chair, hands tucked behind his head, and watched along with Brandt.

On the screen, the window exploded inwards and a man, moving incredibly in ultra slow-motion, landed on his back in the middle of the office.

"Is that Darren?" asked Endo.

"There is no... fucking Hell, Endo, do you want to go out the window as well?"

Endo said that he did not.

"Then shut up about Darren," Brandt said.

On the screen, the man—who was neither Murtow nor Ricks, he realised—removed the thrice-wrapped fire-hose from his waist. Then he appeared to shout something. "Is there no sound to this video?" he asked of Endo.

"Which package do you have?" Endo asked, pausing the video. He was chewing on a liquorice lace now.

"Premium Minus, I think," said Brandt, to which Endo responded with hissings between his teeth. "What, is that one no good?"

"Not if you want to hear what's going on," Endo said. "Premium Minus is essentially Basic Plus, but without the advertisements playing over your footage every twelve minutes. For an extra eighty dollars a month, you would've been able to hear what Darren screamed just then, but as it stands, we're just gonna have to have a guess." He turned back to the screen and played a few frames individually. "Looks like he's saying, 'BAAAAAAAAAAAA!', but that's just my opinion."

"Why the hell would he be saying 'BAAAAAA!'?" By now Brandt was, like Doctor Harold Shipman, beginning to lose his patience.

"Who knows why Darren does *anything*," said Endo, before hitting the play button again.

They watched as the grainy footage showed the man helping himself to the bar. He then went over to Brandt's desk and took up the framed photograph that had been sitting there.

"Holly Generic," said Brandt. "Why's he looking at a picture of one of my women?"

Endo pushed pause. "Is she pretty?" he asked, because if she was, that was his question easily answered.

"Not really," Brandt said. "Face like a robber's dog, really. I forgot that picture was even there. Told Sandra to get rid of it ages ago. Anyway, carry on."

Endo pushed play.

The mystery man put the framed photograph face-down, which Brandt agreed was much better, then began going at the desk drawers as if he owned the place.

What was he searching for? *Whatever it is, he won't find it there*, Brandt thought. The bottom drawer was where he kept his outsized tape-measures and flat batteries for watches he no longer owned.

"Why is it so damn difficult to ignore another man's junk drawer?" Brandt asked.

"It's the mystery," Endo said, still focusing on the screens. "The mystery of finding mysterious items. A mystery of a mystery."

Indeed, Brandt thought, but now he was furious by what he was seeing on the myriad monitors in front of him.

"He's going through my computer! Oh! Is nothing sacred?" And then he realised the computer was password-protected, and he rejoiced momentarily, until he remembered what the password was, and then it was fifty-fifty whether this man, this nocturnal caller, let's call him Darren for now, knew anything of password cracking, that being if 1234 doesn't work, give 5678 a go, and if that's still no good, well, it could be *anything*, really.

Then Brandt remembered something, and suddenly felt very stupid, indeed. Why was he watching this as if he didn't know how it all went? He knew the man had gotten into the computer. He knew this because it was unlocked when he'd arrived at his office less than ten minutes ago. He also knew this as there was a new file—DOG KILLING—added to his records. He also knew that the photograph of Molly Generic had been manhandled, because he'd wondered, not eight minutes ago, why the bloody thing was suddenly face-down.

In fact, the only reason he had come here was to do that bit where the camera zooms in, using technology that doesn't exist quite yet that clears up the picture to the point you can see the pores of whoever it is you're looking it.

That's why he was here. To simply identify Darren!

The rest he already knew.

At least, he thought he knew everything, until Darren read the post-it note, and Brandt went, "Ah."

"Ah, sir?" enquired Endo.

"Yeah, uhm, he read what was on the post-it, knows all about Xavier and the meeting at the docks at midnight, He's probably wondering what the clit is as we speak."

"The clit, sir?" Endo had heard something of its existence, but couldn't attest to it as he'd never seen it with his own two eyes.

"Never mind that now," Brandt said. "Endo, I need you to do that zooming in and cleaning up thing on this man's face—"

"Mr. Brandt, that technology doesn't really exist—

"Just do it, Endo!" Brandt snapped.

So Endo did it somehow, and then took a step back and said, "Wow! It's so clear. UHD 4K image from a single CCTV frame. I've never seen anything like it in my l—

"No one likes a sarcastic prick," Brandt said.

He looked at the face on the screen.

The face looked back.

"Oh, my God!" said Brandt. "That's Jim McLeod."

"I thought his name was Darren," Endo said, unwisely. Then, "Who's Jim McLeod?" to take the edge off his first comment.

"He's NYPD. I took his wife, their money, their kids—who I then trafficked—and I threw Wicksy, his dog, in the canal."

"You threw Wicksy in the canal?" Endo said, shocked. Brandt truly was a sick sonofabitch.

"Endo, do you still have loads of friends who do karate?"

"A little bit racist," Endo said, "but of course I do. What else do you think we get up to."

"I need you to find this man and karate him back to where he came from," Brandt said. "Either that or kill him."

Endo sighed.

Brandt sighed.

First Ricks and Murtow and now McLeod. Like a slippery penis at a rapid-fire wankathon, things were quickly getting out of hand.

"Take care of this for me, Endo," Brandt said. "And I'll make you my number-one baddie sidekick."

With an offer like that, Endo thought, how can I refuse.

He put on his black gi with the yellow stripes running along its arms, called a few dojos, made a few enquiries, gathered a small army, and set out to find the man he called Darren, but everyone else called McLeod.

14

The McMansion on Pacific Palisades belonging to Percival Xavier was a little quieter during the early hours. There were no frolicking girls by the pool, no behemoth beach-balls being bandied by busty beauties. Everyone was still in bed, recovering from the excesses of the previous day, and in some cases, month. You could say what you wanted about international drug lords, so long as they weren't in the room when you said it, but they certainly knew how to throw a party. Not so good at the after-party clean-up, though.

"Look at the state of this place," Rick said, kicking over a grass-beached inflatable lilo to reveal a passed-out brunette. "You'd think they'd have more pride in their home, wouldn't you?"

Murtow nodded. "They don't care, Ricks," he said. "The more money they have, the more reality escapes them."

Both detectives had their weapons drawn as they circumnavigated the mansion. It had come as something of a surprise to both when they had arrived to no fanfare, and no resistance from the double-gate, which was now unmanned and rather easy to climb over, if you knew where to put your feet. Ricks knew where to put his feet, so he had climbed over and unlocked it from his side to let Murtow in.

That had been almost two minutes ago, and they had yet to encounter anyone conscious.

It had been decided—mainly by Ricks, but Murtow was up for it, too—that they had allowed Xavier a free pass yesterday. It had been the druglord's birthday, after all, and if you can't throw a drug-fuelled hooker-fest on your birthday, well, it just didn't bear thinking about. But that had been yesterday, and today was a new day; tomorrow was something of an enigma, but a week on Tuesday looked promising.

"We're gonna bust him in his drawers," Murtow said, sniggering. "He ain't gonna like that."

"Well," said Ricks, putting his back to the wall and peeking around it. "He shouldn't run about the place with a pocketful of drugs." He did a forward roll across the lawn, knocked a garden gnome sideways, and came back to his feet and the vertical plane.

"Hey, Ricks," Murtow whispered as he pushed up alongside him.

"Hm?"

"I just wanted... I just wanted to thank you for what you did this morning. I... I would never have... you know?"

Ricks *did* know. "You're welcome, Reg," he said, and then went back to scouting the place.

The door, the one they had used yesterday that led into the mansion's kitchen, was locked. "Fuckit!" Ricks shouted in a whisper. He hadn't expected the door to open—everyone locks their doors at night, especially those in the middle of criminal activities seeking to keep the cops from calling unannounced—but he was no less peeved now that it wouldn't. "We're gonna have to find another way in," he said, for the obvious needed stating judging by the discombobulated countenance of his partner.

"Hey, Ricks," Murtow whispered, following Ricks around the corner of the mansion as their search for entry continued. They were both keeping low beneath the shrubbery; Ricks's mullet was the only thing visible from across the garden on the other side of the pool, but he wasn't to know that as it was on top of his head, where he always kept it.

"What is it, Reg?" Ricks whispered. "Also, how many times have we gone around this house already? Feels like more than once."

"Not all the way around yet," Murtow said. "Ricks, we didn't have time to talk about it this morning, but did you manage to take that girl out last night? Velma?"

"Velda," Ricks corrected him. "Yeah, we went out." There wasn't much more to add. The date had been a bit of a let-down for Ricks, and it would need to be resolved on the all-important second date, which most definitely wasn't going to be at a Yoko Ono concert on Thursday night. That was sufficient to kill a potential relationship.

"Are you seeing her again?" Murtow asked. He was smiling stupidly, as if the notion of love excited him and this was the first he was hearing of it. But it was more than that, Ricks thought as he stopped shuffling along the endless wall to inspect his partner's face more studiously. And what he saw there upon that big, round, lugubriously smiling face was... pride. Murtow was *proud* of him, and also living vicariously through him—this was also evident on Murtow's face—which Ricks fully understood. It couldn't be much fun, married for decades to the same woman, seven kids off the production line with the possibility of more, even though one of them (and he would get to the bottom of it) was a practising Unabomber. It was no wonder

Murtow wanted to get into the sexy details of his encounter with Ms. Brugenheim.

"She's a captivating woman," Ricks said, which did not answer Murtow's question at all, but Ricks left it there. *Let the old pervert suffer*, he thought.

Ricks moved on once more, Murtow imitated with a sudden inexplicable feeling of dissatisfaction, and presently they arrived at a garage, which had been left open. The collection of cars within—seven of them, there were, all shiny and glittery and cunty—must have amounted to ten-mil in cash-money.

The Acura NSX, in stunning electric blue, is a two-seater, rear-wheel-drive sports car combining a twin-turbo three-point-five-litre V6—

"I will shoot you in the face," Ricks said, "if you don't knock that right off. Why are you even nervous? The only signs of life we've seen so far were that Cosby-teaser under the lilo, and each other."

"I just don't like this, Ricks. This guy Xavier, he's like the guy in movies that's untouchable."

"Well, I'm gonna touch him, Reg. I'm gonna touch him all over."

A smile slowly replaced the uncertainty that had been playing around with Murtow's features. He was either comforted by Ricks's words, or he had wind.

"What's say we hunker down here for a while?" Ricks said, grinning that award-winning smile of his that Murtow hated so much.

"We left the car on the hill out front," Murtow said, sadly. "They'll know we're here."

"That thing doesn't even *look* like a car anymore." And it didn't. It looked like a scrapyard had had a bad dream and, for comfort, climbed into bed with a plane crash. "If anyone drives past it on the way up here, they'll assume it's been abandoned."

"Why don't we just kick the door in?" Murtow asked. "I mean, why don't *you* just kick the door in? The sooner we bust Xavier and his cronies, the sooner we find the clit."

Ricks had almost forgotten about the clit. It's funny how something as important as the clit would slip a guy's mind. Hm.

"We wait," Ricks said, secreting himself between a Tesla Cybertruck and the garage wall.

"Yeah," Murtow said, holstering his six-shooter. "We'll just wait here, let the bad guys come to us."

Outside the garage, the white-hot sun disappeared for a moment behind a cloud that Ricks thought looked uncannily like the Sheraton Hotel logo.

For some reason.

*

The hotel room at the Sheraton was unbearably, insufferably, hellishly hot and McLeod was not, upon waking, in the best of moods. He had slept stark-bollock naked—which was not difficult when you only had to remove two items of clothing to get there—and directly in front of the air-con, but still he awoke, all glazed over with sweat and so denuded of saliva that he couldn't, for the first ten minutes after waking, peel his tongue from the roof of his mouth. The pimply school-leaver that manned (term used loosely) reception would ask him upon checkout if he had slept well, and had everything been to his satisfaction, to which he would reply, "Yes, I slept like a baby, although it's hard not to when the room is so warm there are parrots flying around in it. And yes, everything was to my satisfaction. I specifically ordered a room that would strip me of twelve pounds without any exercise whatsoever."

"Whatever," McLeod said once his tongue was detached. He was up now, cooling down a little by dangling his balls out through the crack in the window that would open no wider thanks to the advent of hotel window restrictors. His ballbag enjoyed the faint breeze it received. Things could only get better from hereon in.

He poured a glass of water from the bathroom faucet and downed it in two gulps. After repeating the process thrice, he put on his uniform—black trousers, dirty white vest, nothing more—and slumped onto the bed, where he ran through the day's plans in his inexplicably sore head.

Firstly, he would head over to THE LOAN WOLF to pick up his pistol, because you can't have a gunfight without a gun (anyone that did so was stupid, and even more stupid if they used bananas instead) and to be entirely truthful, McLeod was sick of being unarmed. He liked the feel of a piece rubbing against the small of his back; currently he was a handgun eunuch, and that had been okay thus far, but things were getting down to the nitty-gritty now. The end was in sight—and not a moment too soon, he thought, because if this were a film, it wouldn't half be dragging on— and would come to a head at the docks at midnight.

It was no surprise that the denouement would take place at the docks. It was the perfect place for shooting, since no one can hear anything for all the boats coming and going. It was big, so there were numerous places to hide, containers to climb on top of, jump down from, all that malarkey. There were swinging things with hooks attached to them, and overhead cranes, and falling containers. It was a John Woo wet dream. All the best action films had explosive scenes at the docks: *The Expendables, The Transporter* (pretty much anything with Jason Statham in it, apparently), *Heist, The Jackal, John Wick, Hanna*, the list goes on.

"Yeh, but this ain't a film, McLeod," he reminded himself. Though it would make a terrific page-turner, the likes of which you could buy at all good bookstores, but mainly from that mysterious place know chiefly, and somewhat ominously, as 'online'.

That last part had been a thought, and not a line of spoken dialogue, though either or neither would have worked just fine.

He stood, went to the bathroom for more water, and it was there he found himself when there came a tapping, as of someone gently rapping, rapping on the fucking door. Since this was a Sheraton hotel and not an Edgar Allen Poe chamber, McLeod said:

"Checkout ain't until eleven." To himself, he added, "Sheraton pricks," unwittingly creating the main antagonist for the inevitable sequel.

"Room service," a woman's voice said. "And also, I'm here to turn down your bed."

McLeod hadn't wanted to scrape the bottom of the barrel so soon, but he couldn't help himself. "You wouldn't be the first woman to turn down my bed, lady!" And then he laughed, and the woman laughed, albeit nervously, which set McLeod's teeth on edge. "I'll just be a moment," he said, searching the bathroom for something—anything!—he could fashion into a weapon. "I'm just... I'm just wiping... my ass... few more should do it..." With a filthy toilet-brush in hand, he came slowly out of the bathroom and edged silently, slowly, toward the door.

"Mr. McLeod, is everything... is everything okay in there?" The woman was scared; her voice had something of a tremor to it, and McLeod thought he heard another voice, a whisper, telling her what to say.

"Everything's fine, lady!" McLeod said, trying to sound as if he were still in the bathroom. The fake echo was probably excessive. "It was just... it was one of those shits where the third wipe is worse than the first, and you start to wonder what the hell is going on, you know?" He knew that she knew. Of course she did. Those shits happen to everyone.

More whispering from the other side of the door, and then the woman said, "Come out without a fight or the woman gets it." Then there came frantic sobbings as the woman pleaded with her captor, who hushed her into silence.

McLeod looked out through the window; even if he could get out—and he couldn't thanks to the sick sonofabitch who'd invented hotel window restrictors—it was a helluva long way down. Too far for any man to fall and not become soup. So that idea was out of the window, which was, thanks to hotel window restrictors, about the only thing that could squeeze through.

He was trapped.

The woman was silently sobbing.

Whoever held her hostage—no doubt one of Brandt's men, come to take care of him before he reached the docks at midnight—wouldn't wait much longer. This was going to happen, whether McLeod liked it or not. And he didn't.

"Okay!" said the vengeful NYPD detective wielding a nugget-encrusted toilet brush. He moved across to the door, reached for the handle, and pushed it down.

It was amazing how quickly twenty-five angry Japanese men could fill a hotel room.

McLeod dropped the toilet brush and started swinging just as...

*

A bullet thunked into the Cybertruck, leaving a slight dent next to where Ricks's mullet had been a moment earlier.

"Where the hell did that come from!" Ricks said, dropping down into a crouch and ushering Murtow deeper into the garage.

"How the hell am I supposed to know?" Murtow shouted, for now there were bullets flying everywhere and it was, unsurprisingly, a tad noisy.

"You were supposed to be keeping a look out!" Ricks said, firing three times back at where he thought one of the shooters might be. "What's the point of being a lookout if you're not very good at looking out?!" Two more shots into oblivion, but Ricks wasn't counting. he had plenty of magazines—a dozen of them in holsters clipped to his belt, two more in his jeans, one in each sock, and one wrapped in a condom tucked up his—

"I never said I was looking out!" Murtow said, firing a single shot at no one in particular. He, unlike Ricks, was keeping count of bullets. With the shot yesterday to take out the rear tyre of the Accord, plus the one he had fired just now, that left... "Hey, Ricks! I hope you don't mind me not shooting back as often as you!"

Ricks unloaded six, seven, eight, nine, ten, eleven times before answering with, "I told you that fucking six-shooter was no good!"

"You didn't tell me shit!" Murtow cried as he ducked for cover behind a Lambo.

Ricks reached into his jeans, and was relieved almost immediately as he came back out with the condom magazine. Clean it was, too, which was a nice, little bonus. He squeezed the magazine out of the prophylactic and slammed it into his gun in that cool way they always do.

"I'll draw fire!" Ricks said. "Cover me, Reg!"

Before Murtow could dissuade Ricks from drawing anything, least of all fire, his partner was gone, running manically up the white-gravel path, shooting at everything that moved and plenty of things that didn't.

Murtow fired once, twice, thrice, and quarce, then the Smith & Wesson Model 19, now spent like a premature ejaculator on a nudist beach, went—

*

Click! went McLeod's kneecap as he was flung across the single bed by one of the Japanese karate-cum-henchmen. He bounced once off the mattress before slamming hard into the fold-down trouser-press.

Bodies lay in varying states of unconsciousness all around the room. Some were on the floor, some leaning against the cupboards. There were two in the bathtub, and one in the shower cubicle that McLeod didn't remember putting there, but he must have.

McLeod jumped back to his bare feet and regarded his opponents the way one might regard a wild chimp. That was to say he knew he was beaten, and any bravado he had left was merely a bluff, in case the chimp had an ounce of heart.

From the twenty-five that had entered Room 1408 of the Sheraton Grand, LA, only four remained. Two of which looked bored; one of them even yawned.

"We can do this all day," said the one at the front. The leader, McLeod thought, or perhaps the only one still standing that could speak English.

"Well *I* can't," McLeod said, dusting himself off. "I've got to check out at eleven."

And that was when he realised he was standing next to the door, and they were across the room, beyond a sea of groaning and moaning bodies and on the other side of the bed.

There was nothing stopping him leaving through the half-open door to his left. But before he went, he had to know.

"Did Brandt send you?"

"Yes," said the one wearing the blackest of black belts. He tightened it, as if he knew somehow, someone out there, was talking about it. "Mr Brandt sends his regards." He dropped into some sort of karate stance that McLeod knew nothing about, and went, "HYAAAA!" It was all a bit cliche, but there you have it.

The other three followed suit, although with about half as much gusto.

"You fight well, Darren," said the leader, still crouching, ready to attack. "It is a shame we have to put an end to you."

Darren? McLeod had been called all manner of things over the years, but this was the first time someone had referred to him as "Darren."

"Look!" McLeod said, pointing toward the window on the other side of the room. "Is that Godzilla?"

The four Japanese men turned their heads in unison. When they turned back, Jim McLeod had—

*

Pissed off to somewhere else, Ricks had, leaving Murtow with zero in the way of bullets and even less in the way of hope.

"Shit!" Murtow said, checking the empty barrel of his six-shooter for some reason, shaking out the spent shells. The gun was useless now, unless he was gifted with a near-distance pistol whip. He holstered it and moved past the yellow Lambo, to where a stack of used tyres reached up to the garage roof.

No one was shooting at him anymore. The shots he now heard were off in the distance. Had Ricks managed to get the shooters away from him, so that he might get away, live to fight another day?

"Your friend left you, did he?" said a voice. Murtow spun around, almost lost his balance, managed to steady himself on a 1950s gas-pump, which had no right being there, but Murtow was glad it had been. The voice had come from the face of a man who now stood just a few feet away from Murtow, and that man was highly trained, it seemed, in the art of creeping around undetected, even though he was twice the size of a professional wrestler and almost as wide as half a gate, for it was none other than the doorman from yesterday's party.

Not the Russian one—Vladisvar—but the one on the left, depending on which side of the gate you were standing.

"I'm too old for this—"

*

"Shit!" Ricks said as he dove twelve feet into the air and came down into a fortunately-placed Forsythia.

Now, it is possible for a man to leap so high, if that man is trained properly and has a proverbial—and, even more helpful, a real—spring in his step. But Ricks, no longer a spring chicken himself, was not trained to launch himself to such great heights. Which is where luck came in.

It is a well-known fact, for those in the know, that trampoline sales increase exponentially whenever an action film is being made. They are essential, nay *compulsory*, on the set of anything starring Schwarzenegger, Stallone, or Smith (Will, not so much Kevin), because a strategically placed trampoline or springboard, usually concealed cleverly behind a wall or a row of shrubs or in a divot, can make all the difference between a good action scene and a great one. If a grenade goes off nearby, and there's a trampoline in the vicinity, it becomes a thing of beauty. Before you know it, men are flying arse over tit, bouncing this way and that, springing over walls, and going, "Ahhaaa!" using the Wilhelm scream as explosions erupt all around and behind them. *Beautiful!* It is practically impossible, therefore, to purchase trampolines or springboards in LA. Harder to find than the clit, some might say. Because all of the trampolines are in use on the lots of Paramount or Fox. Yes, there is one down at the precinct, and the one that killed Ricks's wife, but other than that they are like rocking horse shit, but Percival Xavier had some in his back garden.

Of course he did; he's rich!

Suddenly, machine-gun fire peppered the shrubbery Ricks was hiding amongst. Leaves rained down like confetti, and Ricks took to his back to avoid going the way of the greenery.

When the firing stopped, Ricks waited for three seconds—which meant he went on two—before rolling out into the clear and firing a single shot in the direction of the shooter.

As luck would have it, as it so often does in these situations, the bullet penetrated the machine-gunner's eye-socket without much effort. A flower of crimson blossomed in slow-motion behind the bad guy's head, and the poor fella didn't even have the chance to Wilhelm scream before he slumped dramatically—*melodramatically*, Ricks thought; the bad guy certainly not in the running for an Oscar any time soon, or ever, really—to the grass.

Ricks was about to celebrate his stroke of luck when more gunshots came at him from the rear. Back into the shrubbery he went, because, as everyone knows, it not only looks great in any garden or park area, but it's also, to an extent, bulletproof.

A bullet whipped past Ricks's ear, so closely it went *Whizzzpppp!* and Ricks said, "Oh now you're—"

*

"Really starting to get on my tits!" said yesterday's doorman as he slammed Murtow up against the garage wall one more time. Blood now seeped from the corner of Murtow's mouth, which was never a good sign. He doubled over, and then somehow *trebled* over, which confused both he and the man currently pummelling him.

"Where's Xavier!?" Murtow said, spitting blood and coughing violently. Was this the end? *Can't be*, Murtow thought, for they had yet to set foot on the docks. "You don't have to do this. Just tell me where he is and—"

The wind was knocked from him as a sledgehammer fist was driven into his stomach. He felt his guts separate; his kidneys had never *been* so far apart.

Which made him think of Ricks. He and his new partner had been inseparable since the captain paired them up all those hours ago. And now here they were, forced apart, Murtow fighting for his life, Ricks doing whatever it was that Ricks was doing.

Just like his kidneys, he and Ricks had become, for want of a better word—or more expensive and extensive thesaurus—*uncoupled*, and for the first time since they'd gotten together, Murtow felt...

*

"Single!" McLeod breathlessly said, boarding the bus and slamming a coin he'd just found down on the little tray between himself and the driver. The driver looked down at the coin as if it had just taken a shit on his nonna's head.

"That's not enough," he said. "Also, it's forty fucking French Francs."

McLeod picked up the coin and turned it over to check it. It *was*. It was forty fucking French Francs, a coin not legal in France, and never legal in America, since 2002. "It must be worth something," said McLeod. "More than the cost of a bus ticket, I reckon. Why don't you keep the forty Francs and I'll go and sit down?"

"This ain't the Antiques Roadshow!" said the driver, who was looking increasingly like the late, great Bernie Mac as the time passed. "Dollar seventy-five, or get yo' ass off my bus."

"Yeah, get off the bus!" said one of its riders. A little old lady wearing too much make-up and not enough clothes for someone of her age.

"Get off, man," said another. "I got places to be."

"Hands up who wants him off the bus?" added a third person, this one nondescript, save for a blur of a face and a suggestion of a body.

"Who are *you* to start a poll?" an irate fourth asked the blurry poll-starter. "Who died and made you King of the bus?"

"I'm the King of this bus," said the driver. "Ain't no one taking my crown."

The whole bus broke out in argument over whether or not to remove McLeod physically, or let him ride for free.

"Ain't no one ride for free on my motherfucking bus," the driver said. "Y'all better know that before you start makin' up the damn rules as you go along."

It was quite the kerfuffle now, and threatened to become physical when one of the passengers, the little old lady with too much make-up and not enough clothes, threw an arthritic fist at no one in particular.

McLeod had had enough of this nonsense, and turned to disembark the silly bus, but there was now a Japanese man—yes, that one!— standing between McLeod and the street.

"Get off the bus, Darren," said Endo. McLeod didn't know that was his name for certain, but it was printed, in nice cursive font—*Weddingday Regular*, perhaps—across the left breast of the man's gi.

McLeod sighed. The people of the bus fell silent. "Why do you keep calling me Darren!" he said, and he threw a punch into Endo's face, knocking him back off the steps of the bus. Endo did an involuntary backward roll, and then bounced up a bit because someone was in the process of moving a trampoline.

"Drive!" McLeod bellowed at the driver.

"I ain't goin' nowhere with yo' ass still—"

Then there came a rapping, as of three Japanese karatemen clambering all over the roof of the bus, and the driver pushed the button that closed the noisy hydraulic doors and put his foot to the floor.

Everyone on board flew back into the bus, including McLeod, who managed to grab hold of one of the poles.

"Get the fuck off me!" said the pole, whose full name was Andrzej Bartosz.

McLeod apologised and turned his attention to the roof, upon which all four survivors of the Sheraton 1408 brawl now danced and staggered to keep themselves aboard. Just like that mercury motherfucker from *Terminator 2*, they weren't going to stop coming for him until he was dead.

"What should I do, man?" the driver said. He was speaking to McLeod directly, and he looked nervous.

"Just keep on going!" McLeod said. "They can't get on as long as we don't stop."

He turned and gazed dramatically off into nothingness, as if cameras might be on him and he didn't want to come across as an amateur.

"Whatever you do," he said, pausing for effect, "don't let this bus drop below—"

*

Thirty, Ricks thought solemnly to himself. Thirty years old, and this was how he was going to die.

He was surrounded on all sides now. Had it not been for the Portaloo at the back of the mansion—which wasn't as bulletproof as the Forsythia, but beggars can't be choosers—he'd already be dead.

"LAPD! We only want to speak to your boss!" Ricks shouted, his voice echoing all around the interim shitter. "Why do you want to protect that asshole anyway?"

There came a temporary ceasefire, and then a solitary little voice said, "The pay's pretty good."

"Yeah!" said another voice. This one off to Ricks's right, but it was difficult to tell from within the mobile toilet. "The pay's good, and we get two weeks off in the summer!"

"That's right!" said the first voice. "Plus, free drugs on the last Sunday of the month!"

"Within reason!" the second voice corrected him.

"Yeah!" said the first, suitably corrected. "Within reason. So long as we don't take the piss!"

Ricks reloaded his Beretta and shook the sweat from his head before wringing out his mullet the way one might a pair of swimming shorts. Then he had a quick wee—when in Rome—and prepared himself for his *Butch and Sundance* moment.

Only he was all alone. He had left *his* Sundance to fend for himself, with only a handful of bullets, which wasn't a very Butch thing to do. But then he realised there wouldn't have been room for the both of them in the Portaloo, anyway, and felt instantly better about leaving Murtow where he was.

"You know backup's on its way!" Ricks said. "LAPD don't take too kindly to people shooting at their detectives."

"You didn't call for backup!" said the first voice. "We saw the state of your car coming up the hill. The radio in that thing is all in pieces."

"I still have my phone!" Ricks said, reaching into his pocket to discover he didn't still have his phone. It must have fallen out while he was doing all those unnecessary gymnastics on the lawn.

"What? This phone?" said the first voice. "Hey, nice profile picture. She's beautiful!"

"That's my dead wife!" Ricks said.

"Why's her head so flat?"

"Trampoline accident," Ricks said, wishing he'd never taken the damn post-mortem pic now. It was a little weird; even the coroner said so, and there are none weirder than those guys.

"Ain't no backup coming!" said the second voice. "You guys are dead! Now, you've got until the count of three to get out here. We're setting up the big gun, you know? It's like that one Blain uses in *Predator*, but bigger!"

"Your three or my three?" Ricks asked, although it didn't really matter.

"That doesn't really matter!" said the first voice, although his confusion was easily discernible. "Just... just get out here with your hands up, and we promise we'll kill you quickly."

Ricks considered this and frowned. "So, I stay in here and I die quickly with that big noisy gun of yours, or I come out and you take me to somewhere to kill me quickly. Is that... is that what you're trying to say?"

"I don't bloody know!" said the first voice.

Just then, and unannounced, a new voice came, and although it was new to the conversation, Ricks recognised it instantly.

"There will be no quick killing today!" Percival Xavier said. "Detective Ricks, I should imagine it's getting ever-so-warm in there, hmm? Yes, Porta-Johns are not the nicest of places to be when the sun is blazing down such as it is. I should think you are sweating by now, am I correct?"

"Like Mel Gibson in a synagogue," Ricks said, for he was. And panting, as well.

"And you would like, perhaps, a way out of there that didn't involve the big gun?" Xavier said, and was that a little snigger Ricks heard? The sonofabitch was enjoying this.

"I'm gonna end you, Xavier!" Ricks said, wiping sweat from his eyes and wishing that whoever had used this place last had checked it had all gone down. "Murtow and me, we'll—"

"You mean *this* Murtow?" Xavier said, and now he laughed loudly, but only for a few seconds because it was Murtow's line next.

"Hey, Ricks!" he said. "Don't do what this sonofabitch wants! You hear me? Kill his—"

Ricks recognised the sound that stopped Murtow from going on. It was a pistol whip to the back of the head, and quite a heavy one, from the sounds of it. It had to be to silence Murtow who, once he got going, could rant with the best of them. Whoever *them* are.

"Don't you hurt him!" Ricks bellowed. He was angry, now, with Murtow for getting himself caught and with himself for leaving him back in the garage. And now here he was, stuck in a two-by-two shit-stinking sauna while his partner was out there, being beaten about the back of the head with a pistol, and it was all Ricks's fault. Well, at least some of it was. They could argue about which bits were the fault of whom later. If there indeed was to be a later. "I'll... I'll come out if you let him go."

There was an uncomfortable silence that went on for an interminable amount of time—that was, in fact, thirteen seconds that felt more like months to Ricks—but it was, Ricks thought, a wholly unnecessary quietude. He knew they weren't going to let Murtow go. They were both already dead.

"I'll make sure Murtow makes it to his retirement party," Xavier said, finally.

Ricks considered this carefully; it was one of those answers, ambiguous at best, which could mean several things. He didn't say Murtow would be *alive* at the party, for starters.

Ricks had no choice, though, and he knew it. "Okay," he said. "But I want it in writing, signed and notarised, that Reginald Murtow will not be harmed." He tucked his gun into the waistband of his jeans and slid the plastic lock across. "I'm coming out."

No sooner had he stepped foot out of the portable toilet than something hard and heavy came down on the back of his—

*

"Head for the 2nd Street Tunnel!" McLeod instructed the driver, who was sweating profusely now as he'd never gone over forty miles-per-hour in a built-up area. It was absolutely crazy! He would surely be fired by the end of the day, if in fact he survived that long.

"But that tunnel is only twelve-and-a-half-feet high at its entrance," said the driver, whose name was Vernon. McLeod saw it on the license hanging in front of him.

"Yeah?" McLeod said. "I know it is."

The four Japanese men on the roof were still stomping about up there, trying to find a way in and generally making a nuisance of themselves.

"But this bus is just a little shorter than... ooh! I get it now!"

He gets it now, McLeod thought. Vernon was apparently one of the smarter people on the bus. The others were still arguing about whether to evict McLeod, oblivious to the fact they were under siege (not to be confused with the film of the same name, featuring that fat guy, Putin's mate, Seagull, and whatnot).

"Just keep us going in a straight line all the way to the tunnel," McLeod said. "You're doing a great job, Vernon."

"If I was doing a great job," Vernon said, steering the bus through the traffic and knocking aside anyone unfortunate enough to be going slower than the bus, "I'd be saying, 'Where would you like me to put the sun-cream next, Ms Knowles?'"

"That *would* be a great job," McLeod said, drifting into deep thought for a second. "Anyway, keep up the good work. Give her a little shake every now and then," he said, "try to jiggle them off."

"Why are those men after you?" the feisty old lady said. McLeod still didn't know her name, since she didn't have an LA bus license dancing around her head the way Vernon did. It would have been a lot easier if she did, McLeod thought. "Why are they... on the roof of this bus... chasing you?"

McLeod didn't want to frighten the little old lady any more than she already was, so he said, "Have you ever thought it might be *you* they're after?" And left it at that.

Andrzej Bartosz, who was a lanky thing with slinky arms and a wig that said, "Pick on me! Please, pick on me!" well, that guy blocked McLeod in the aisle and said something unpleasant in Polish.

"Listen, I know the air's thinner up where you are, so this might be difficult for you to understand, but I'm not the bad guy here. A guy named Brandt is the bad guy. Those men up there—" he pointed up to where, unseen to those in the bus, the four Japanese men skittered this way and that, doing everything they could to stay aboard, "—are his henchmen. I'm an NYPD detective and I'm here to take Brandt down before—"

"He's not wearing any socks and shoes!" the old lady said, pointing to McLeod's bare feet. "You can't get on a bus without socks and shoes on. That's... well that's just mad!"

McLeod held his hands up. "Look, the shoes and socks thing is just, well, it's just something that I do."

"And that vest's riffy," said the lady. "More holes than a female-only orgy in a Swiss cheese—"

"Hey, McLeod!" Vernon suddenly interrupted. "We've got a little problem here!"

McLeod turned from the irritated (and irritating!) throng and returned to the front of the bus. "What's the problem, Vern... Oh, I see."

"Yeah," said the driver.

Endo, if indeed that was his name or just the name of the company that makes the suits, had lowered himself down the front of the bus and was now, with his face all mushed up and his eyeballs pressed against the glass, signalling Vernon to either pull the bus to the side of the road, where this could be dealt with amicably and without further ado, or otherwise he would die, and McLeod would die, and they would all die together, and wouldn't that be a terrible tragedy for everyone involved.

"What's he say?" Vernon asked, for lip-reading was not his forte at the best of times, let alone when it was in Japanese.

"I don't know, man," McLeod said. "Just... turn on the windshield wipers, get him off there."

"He ain't a spot of rain, McLeod!" Vernon said. "Wipers ain't gonna get him offa there like some dead ol' bug!"

"Then just keep going," McLeod said. He put his elbow through the little red box which said to break the glass if you wanted to have a play with the miniature hammer inside. It wasn't a gun, but it would have to do, and it was certainly better than a toilet brush. Like in an FPS videogame, he was upgrading slowly, and at least he hadn't had to start off with just a knife, the way they always do. "We're almost at the bridge. I want everyone in their seats, you hear me? Asses on seats, that means you too, Giraffeszky!"

He seemingly didn't like being ordered around, but the Polish man sat down as instructed. Never argue with a man holding a miniature bus hammer, that's what his mother always told him, and she was right. That thing was small enough to take someone's eye out or bruise a knuckle or two. That thing was terrifying.

With everyone in their seats, some still complaining about McLeod's continued presence, others moaning that they'd missed their stop, McLeod said, "This'll all be over in a few minutes, okay? You'll all be able to get back to your normal day, and—"

Suddenly, a pair of legs were wrapped around McLeod and a sweaty asshole rubbed up and down his neck and shoulders. It was horrible. Unless you were into that sort of thing, which McLeod definitely wasn't.

"One of them's getting in through the 'scape hatch!" the old lady proffered, and she was right. They'd figured out the way into the bus was through the emergency escape hatch in the roof of the bus. "You'd have thought they'd have tried that ages ago."

Everyone on board agreed with her, except McLeod, who was trying to push the karate-man back up through the hatch, and also, quite importantly, continue to breathe. "Son... bitch... choking... gnnnhhh."

The man's legs tightened even more, but no one seemed to want to help McLeod, who was trying to use the little hammer on his assailant's shins. It was altogether fruitless, though. If anything, it was denting the hammer.

"Everyone hold on!" came the cry from the front of the bus, and all eyes turned to Vernon and the dark tunnel up ahead.

The bus sped up even more.

Vernon muttered, "If they gon' fire my ass, I'm gon' give them a damn good reason to!"

"Aaaagh!" screamed almost everyone at once.

The old lady said, "Ooh, I don't like this one bit."

Andrzej Bartosz yelled, "Cholera!" as loud as he could, which wasn't too much of a terrible curse word, and his mother wouldn't have minded in the slightest.

Then the bus went dark. And the tap-dancing Japanese men on the roof fell instantly silent, perhaps because two-and-a-half of them were now a permanent fixture of the 2nd Street tunnel's entrance, at least until they were sponged off. The bus was only in the tunnel for seconds. When light returned as they exited the tunnel, they all wished it hadn't.

The man who was now just half-a-man was still wrapped around Mcleod, though McLeod now wore him like a scarf. There was blood spraying everywhere, not to mention all the giblets hanging down from the emergency escape hatch, like decorations from Ed Gein's fortieth birthday party. When he realised what had happened, McLeod threw the man's bottom half into an empty seat across the bus.

The bus screeched to a halt; the smell of burnt rubber suddenly filled the place up.

"Is he going to be okay?" asked a dark-haired woman, who McLeod was only just seeing for the first time (probably due to cuts in the budget, or something). She was looking at the half-a-man and making the sign of the cross in-between gags.

"I think he's dead," said Andrzej, searching for a pulse, which was harder than it looked with just a pair of legs and a groin.

"He might not *die*, you know," said the little old lady, popping a Werther's Original into her mouth and giving it a helluva suck. "There was a girl yesterday, some TokTiker, I don't know... got 'erself chopped in half, and she's doing well. Sold 'er story to the magazines and everything. For half pay, no doubt."

"He's dead," McLeod said, ignoring the old lady completely, for he had located the place where there would have been a pulse, and it just wasn't pulsing.

"This one up here's still alive," said Vernon.

McLeod turned, wiped his bloody hands, and yet a clean little hammer, on his filthy vest, and said, "Endo," in that cool voice they always use when the proverbial is about to strike the machine with the rotating blades.

McLeod stood and walked toward the doors. He was going to take care of Endo, send a message to Brandt that would tell him he's messed with the wrong man this time. Brandt would shudder whenever the name McLeod came up, but that was all academic, really, because he was still going to assassinate the baddie on the docks at midnight, and he wouldn't, unfortunately, have that much time to be afeared.

"Is he gettin' off, now?" asked the old lady.

"Hey!" said Andrzej, "you can't just leave your half-a-man here."

McLeod didn't hear them as he climbed down the steps on the side of the bus, about to take part in the most epic fight since—

"He ran off!" a passing postman said. "Went that way, but he was running pretty fast, and you don't look like you have it in you." He motioned to McLeod's raggedy framework, and he was quite right, so McLeod didn't bonk him on the head with his little hammer.

"Ran off, did he?" McLeod said, rhetorically. If McLeod hadn't been walking down the aisle of the bus in super slow-motion, Endo wouldn't have had a chance of getting away, but he had, so that was that. "Well," he said.

And he took to his heels, leaving the hissing bus with its bloody roof and its several caricatures behind him, for he had a pawn shop to visit, because that was where the guns—

*

Were you expecting another clever transition back to Ricks and Murtow? Nope, this chapter's gone on for far too long. Time to start a new one.

15

"That's excellent news!" Brandt said, filling the room with blue smoke from one of his green cigars rolled on the thighs of exotic brown ladies. "I knew those pricks wouldn't be able to keep their beaks out of this."

"You want me to kill them now, or do you want to be there—"

"Xavier, you are getting ahead of yourself," said Brandt, crushing the cigar out and taking a furtive sip of scotch. "I don't just want to be there when Ricks and Murtow die. I want to be the one to pull the trigger."

"Well, that's a bummer," Xavier said, lugubriously. Brandt could almost smell his sulking. "I was quite looking forward to it."

Brandt huffed. He didn't usually negotiate with people lower than he, and there were few higher, but Xavier had been the one to capture the annoying cops, so there was that.

"I'll tell you what," he said, waving a hand in the direction of Mac the Bartender to let him know his glass was almost empty. "Since we're meeting at the docks tonight at midnight to surreptitiously welcome this massive shipment of clit into the country, and therefore into my possession—and a little bit of it will be yours, of course—why not bring them to the party and we'll do it there?"

"Are you sure that's a good idea, Mr. Brandt?" Xavier enquired. "Most things go awry at the docks after dark. It's a well-known trope and—"

"If you want to shoot one of them, while I shoot the other, then bring them to the docks." It was no longer an idea; it was an order. "We can celebrate after with a clit party."

"I'm not sure we should call it that," Xavier glumly mumbled. "Might attract the wrong type."

"Yes, yes, you're probably right," Brandt said as he accepted a fresh glass of liquid hell from the part-time bartender before waving him rudely off. "So, we have a deal, then? You, me, LAPD's finest, soon to be dead, and the drugs, midnight at the docks."

He didn't wait for Xavier to answer before hanging up.

"Fucking prick."

*

"Fucking prick," Xavier said, realising he'd been hung up on. He dropped the phone into its cradle and said, to anyone close enough to hear, "And is there any chance we can upgrade to a phone without a cradle? What is this, the fucking seventies?"

"It's for dramatic effect," Vladisvar said, for he had returned, despite earlier assurances that he wouldn't. "When you end a conversation, you can slam a phone down into its cradle. It is good, yes? Makes a point. You can't do that with a mobile phone. Breaks the screen."

"Yes, thank you for that, Vlad," Xavier said. "Would your face break if I slammed it down onto this desk?"

Vladisvar shrugged. "Probably," he said, quietly. "It would depend on—"

His associate, the one who normally stands on the left, depending on which side of the gate you are on, gave the big Russian a furtive kick to the shin.

"How are our cops doing?" Xavier asked. "Not passing out just yet, I hope."

"The white one has quite the mouth on him," Vladisvar said. "Anyone would think he was into the torture thing. Keeps asking for it harder, harder, you're gonna make me—"

Another kick to the shin.

"I'm going to tell them the good news," Xavier said, leaving the room. The two big henchmen silently followed, occasionally swapping a glance that said, *Only one of us is going to make head henchman, and it ain't gonna be you!*

The basement was huge. A massive chamber of mainly-empty space intersected with other, less threatening-looking areas. Over to the right, as you came down the always-wet (for some reason) stairs was a carpeted area, with toys scattered across its carpet and a small plastic slide in the corner. Children, three of them, no older than four, giggled and babbled as they ran about the place, throwing plastic balls—overflow from the ball-pit—at each other. This was where those who worked for Xavier could drop their kids off for the day before going out to work. Lovely little space it was, too, although the attached petting zoo had, Xavier opined, been a moment of madness on his part.

The Costa Coffee off to the right thankfully countered the shitty smell from the petting zoo, and was always a great place to grab a regular latte or grande cappuccino while you were torturing. Not just content with Costa Coffee owning the one of the biggest roasteries in Europe, it is also one of the most sustainable buildings in the world and responsibly sources all their raw coffee beans from one-hundred-percent Rainforest Aliance Certified—

"For fuck's sake, Reg!" Ricks said. They were hanging upside down, so his voice came out a little funny, as they always do when suspended in an upended manner. "Now is not the time."

Murtow apologised. "Sorry, man. I think the blood's gone to my head too much. Everything's fuzzy, Ricks. I've passed out so many times, I can smell colours. We're gonna die, Ricks. Upside down like pigs in a slaughterhouse."

"We're not gonna die," Ricks said, knowing that they probably were. "They would have killed us by now if they'd wanted us dead."

"You have to admit," said Murtow, "that things are not looking too good."

Just then, a four-year-old with a miniature plastic cup came along and said, "Do you want a drink, mister?"

Murtow sighed. He knew the little cunt didn't have any water in that cup. It was just a game, and Murtow had played along the first three times, but now, "Fuck off, you fucking goblin!" he said, and the child ran away, crying, spilling invisible water all over the basement floor as he went.

"Great work there, Uncle Reggie," Ricks said, swinging slowly past in his efforts to escape. "No wonder the kids love you."

"Hey, you don't... you don't get to criticise my parenting style," said Murtow, slowly swinging the other way. Chains rattled as they both went. "My six kids—"

"Seven."

"My seven have turned out just fine, and you know why they turned out just fine, Ricks?"

"Because none of them ever tried to give you invisible water in a plastic cup while you hung upside-down in a torture factory?"

Murtow nodded in that awkward way you do when you're upside down. "That's right," he said. "And also because of respect, Ricks. They *respect* their father."

"I'll bet you can't name all of them," Ricks said, bouncing off Murtow and spinning him a little in the opposite direction. Imagine, if you will, two suspended cocoons blowing gently in a midsummer breeze. Now replace those cocoons with sweaty, sweary, ziptied LAPD detectives and you're not too far away.

"Name them?" Murtow said. "My own kids?"

"Yeah!"

"Of course I can name them, Ricks. You think I don't know the names of my own children?"

"Go ahead."

"I'll do it."

"Go on, then."

And so he did. "There's Rhiannon and Ricky, and Carter... and, um, there's Brianna, and, the one with the seizures... erm, whatshisname... Elijah!" He swung back and for a moment came face-to-face with Ricks, who was grinning that annoying grin of his. "Hey, man, I got five!" he said.

"Five out of seven," Ricks said. "Not bad. Not father-of-the-year worthy, but not bad for a man with a head full of blood."

"Gentlemen!" said a voice as it descended the stone steps of the basement. "I trust you are having fun down here?"

"Beautiful!" Ricks said. "I've had worse Airbnbs, though you might want to get those kids checked over by a nit-nurse, other than that, it's fine."

191

Xavier walked slowly across the dingy, dank room. He was, Ricks saw, flanked by his two big henchmen, Vladisvar and oojamacallit. "Hey," Ricks said to the Russian. "Shouldn't you be standing on the other side? You can't have pepper and salt, you know."

"It is because you are upside down," said the Russian. My colleague and I are standing in the right order. It is you who is, how you say, backwards."

He punched Ricks once in the midriff, and the wind exploded from him, reminding him to keep his mouth shut. It hurt like a sonofabitch.

"Are you going to punch your one, Terry?" Vladisvar asked his colleague. It was a great way to shoehorn the second henchman's name in without making it too obvious.

"Yes, Terry," added Xavier, taking a step back. "Why don't you give Detective Murtow a sound pummelling, Terry, whose name we all know is Terry, now."

So the second henchman, Terry—the one who stands on the left of the gate depending on which side of the gate you are standing, and also, as recently discovered, depending upon whether you are the right side up or upside down—gave Murtow a heavy thwack to the kidney. He swung away for a moment and then returned, the way they often do. But now Murtow's face was all scrunched up in pain, and he drooled like Denzel during his King Kong monologue in—

"Don't you hit him!" Ricks cried, trying desperately to free himself of his shackles. Chains rattled, but it was no use. Of course it was no use, he wasn't fucking Harry Houdini. "He's too old for this shit!"

"Ah," Xavier said, "seems as though we've found a weak spot. Detective Ricks here doesn't like to see his partner in pain."

"Take it out on me, you sonofabitch!" Ricks said, hoping they didn't. "He's an old man. Take it out on me!"

Xavier tilted his head so that he could see Ricks's face the right way up, the way it should have been and the way it was, normally. "You would do that to protect your partner?"

Ricks thought about this for a second as he chewed frantically on his day-old gum. He was already in quite a bit of pain, and he wasn't certain he could take too much more himself. "I would," he said, defiantly.

To Vladisvar, Xavier said, "Bring out the electrocutor thingamajig with the spongey, wet attachment."

"You can do him first!" Ricks suddenly said, changing his mind about being brave and nodding in Murtow's direction. "But put it on a low setting. His diaper's already full."

16

McLeod rushed breathlessly into THE LOAN WOLF, sweat dripping from every pore and giving him a generally shiny aspect. His bald head reflected the sun as he entered, sending the proprietor, Oxford Manning, diving for cover behind the counter, as he had mistaken the sudden appearance of light as a thermal flash, the likes of which were usually followed by a rather warm blast and immediate death, for nuclear war was no joke for anyone, except for those dropping the bomb or at a safe distance from where it detonates, in which case it's probably hilarious.

"Oxford!" McLeod shouted, glancing around the shop and seeing no one amongst, between, under, or behind the tat and stolen goods stacked all about the place. "It's me, Ox, McLeod."

"McLeod!" said the proprietor, his head appearing from behind the counter just before the rest of him. When he was fully standing in the vertical plane once again, he said, "I thought you were a bomb."

"I *am* the bomb," McLeod said, and left it at that. "You still got what we discussed over the phone?" He was transfixed by objects on display in the glass counter. There were Rolexes and gold rings, chunky chains and diamond rings. And then there was a boombox, the kind that was all the rage in the early nineties. McLeod kind of liked it, and might have made an offer on it, had he not been travelling light this trip. "Business going well, Ox?" McLeod asked. Rhetorical, of course.

"You know me, Jim," Oxford said. "Trying to do my best to help people out. Lots of debt out there. Lots of it. More than I can afford to take on, of course, but I do my bit to put cash into the hands of those that need it most."

"You're a thieving bastard, Ox," McLeod said. "If it were down to me you'd be working the tuck-shop in Sing-Sing."

"Hey, I'm just trying to make a living—"

"The gun, Ox. I'm only here for the gun and the duct tape."

Oxford nodded and headed into the back room, where he kept the stuff that wasn't for sale or had already been sold. He continued to talk, even though McLeod couldn't see him.

"I heard you've been having some troubles in New York, Jim," he said. "Something about your wife being taken off your hands, and all your money, and your kids being taken and then sold to traffickers, and then your dog being tossed in the canal. I thought, that can't be true; there's no way Jim McLeod would let that happen. He loves Wicksy."

"News travels fast, Ox," McLeod said, lighting a cigarette. Lord knows where it came from, since his pants pockets had been empty up until now. Probably the same place his wallet would come from in a moment. Continuity errors work in mysterious ways.

"I *did* love that dog," McLeod said, blowing out smoke. "She was the mother to my kids, Ox."

And they both laughed.

"No, seriously," McLeod went on, morosely, which brought the mood crashing back down, "that dog was all I had left after Molly came here and the kids moved to Albania."

"Last I heard she was working in a strip club over in Silver Lake," Oxford said from his special room. "*The Dripping Lollipop*, or something."

"Sounds like Molly to me," McLeod said glumly. "She might have a face like a plate of spaghetti, but that body did things for me, Ox. It was enough for me to marry her."

"Hey, you should go and see her," said the proprietor. "You know, while you're in the area. Just know that she only accepts twenties. You toss a dollar at her, they'll haul you out of there quicker than you can recite your vows again."

Upmarket, she'd gone. His ex-wife Molly Generic, slaying the stage with a face like that?

"Nah," McLeod said. "I've got something to take care of, then I'm heading back to New York. Just hope that something cool happens on the flight back, you know? Terrorists, or something. That would be cool."

Oxford Manning reappeared, and now he was carrying a shoebox with McLeod's name scribbled across its lid in Sharpie.

"All these years," McLeod said as he watched the pawnbroker set the box down on the counter. "All these years and you still don't know how to spell my last name."

"I had a go at it, didn't I?" Oxford said, pointing at the scribblings. "See? It's not my fault the Z is silent."

McLeod let that one go, and simply took the lid off the box. He took out the piece—a Glock 20, known to those that know as the "bear killer", due to its power and accuracy—and gave it a quick once-over. "Where did you manage to get this from, anyway?" It was a damn good question.

"Ah, some woman brought it in a few weeks back. She was gonna shoot her husband, you know? Thought the guy was cheating on her, but turned out he wasn't. He was just reconnecting with a long-lost sister, or something, I don't know."

"So, she didn't shoot him?"

"Oh, she still shot him," Oxford said. "*And* the sister. Didn't find out what was really going on until it was too late. Had to get rid of the gun pretty darn quick, so I offered her fifty bucks and a ticket out of town. I wonder if she ever did make it to Canada."

"Nice story," McLeod said, taking two magazines out of the box. *Sluts over 40* and *Schoolgirl Desires*, they were. Oxford quicky snatched them out of McLeod's hands.

"Don't know how they got in there," he said, embarrassedly.

"It was for a cheap magazine gag," said McLeod, and now he did take out two magazines. "Only ten rounds in each?"

"Minus three in that one," said Oxford.

"Three?" McLeod said. "I thought you said she shot her husband and his sister." McLeod wasn't great at maths, but even he knew that made two.

"Tried to shoot herself after," Oxford said. "Think it must have done something to her head, which explains why she brought the gun to me. Should have seen the state of her face. And you thought Molly was ugly."

"Makes sense," McLeod said. "Girl couldn't have been in the right frame of mind to be extorted so badly, right Ox?"

He pushed one of the magazines into the Glock and put the other in his pocket.

"Do I know who it is you're going to be using that thing on?" asked Oxford, tentatively.

"The less you know, the better," said McLeod, because that was the kind of ambiguous, smarmy, sleazy sonofabitch he was, and that would never change.

"Can I ask you one thing then, before you go on this mini-crusade of yours?"

"If it's about the dirty vest and the bare feet," McLeod said, "you needn't bother."

"Shit, Jim, I already know about that. You've had that foot fetish since you were a kid. And the vest makes you look hard, like you're the main character, and you like the way people stare at you when you're wearing it, because they have no idea what's going on, but whatever it is, it must be bad, and you are the one to fix it, all because you're barefoot, bleeding, dirty, and wearing that vest. I've known you long enough."

"Then what is it?" McLeod wanted to get back to work. It was a helluva walk to the docks, and he wanted to get there before it all kicked off at midnight. For some strange reason, he'd been put off using the bus.

"I was just wondering what this is for," said Oxford, taking the duct tape from the shoebox.

That," said McLeod as he turned around and pulled his vest up to reveal a filthy, sweaty back, and also a tattoo of Squirtle, his favourite Pokémon, "is so that you can tape the Glock to my back before I go."

17

Ricks and Murtow were manhandled from the back of a truck and into the night by Vladisvar and Terry, who seemed to be happy that they had been given far larger roles than intended and were making the most of it by overacting whenever the opportunity presented itself.

"Looks like it's almost the end for you two geezers," Terry said, spitting on the floor.

"Execution on the docks!" said Vladisvar with a thicker-then-usual Russian accent. "I'll bet you never saw that coming, huh?"

Ricks, whose wrists were still ziptied behind his back, said, "Actually, we kind of guessed which direction this was going."

"Yeah," said Murtow as Terry nudged him a little too roughly and he fell to his knees. "Once we knew your boss was expecting some clit tonight, it had to be the docks."

"Had to be," added Ricks.

"Yeah, well, once our boss's boss arrives," Vladisvar said, picking up Murtow and pushing him up alongside Ricks, "it's bullets to the back of the heads for you two."

Ricks frowned. So Xavier wasn't the main bad guy? It made sense, for he sounded nothing like the twisted motherhumper who'd had them doing laps of Echo Park the previous day. Ricks was only just realising this was so much bigger than he'd initially thought. If Xavier had a boss, then who the hell was he?

"Just keep limping forwards in that awkward way you are doing," Terry said, pressing the barrel of a gun into Murtow's spine. "And don't try any funny business. Those zipties are very good quality."

"Ten dollars for a thousand of them," said Vladisvar.

"That's right," Terry added. "No expense spared here, despite already exceeding the budget."

The Port of Los Angeles was, for want of a better word, or words, fucking massive, with more terminals than Dignitas. Even at a quarter to midnight it was all hustle and bustle, with ships arriving and leaving, containers being shifted from pillar to post, and people rushing frantically about the place, ticking things off clipboards and shouting in foreign languages. Everywhere you looked there was a Maersk container, or an NYK. There was a distinct stench of oil in the air, thick and acrid with undertones of plastic.

"Knock it off, Reg," Ricks said. "Undertones of plastic, indeed."

"I can't help it, Ricks," Murtow said. "I've never been this close to death before. Turns out my annoying description habit doesn't just come before a bust."

They were nudged forwards toward a brick building, from which huge silver extractors protruded, noisily humming and thrumming and generally making it hard to concentrate. You couldn't do a crossword there. Not because it was too noisy, but because there was a big sign hanging on the building's wall that said, "Absolutely No Crosswords."

Once inside, Ricks suddenly felt cut off from the rest of the world. While it was noisy without, it was remarkably quiet within. Not quiet enough to hear a pin drop, but why would anyone be dropping pins at this time of night, anyway?

A desk had been set up in the middle of the building, which was filled with pallets and boxes and bits of huge machinery that either did something or didn't, depending on whether they were plugged in, or weren't. Behind the desk sat a man that neither Ricks nor Murtow recognised, but they knew the lanky sonofabitch standing just behind him. Percival Xavier had had a change of clothes since the last time they saw him. The suit he now wore looked about two sizes too big for him, as if it were his first day at a new school. His grin suggested he ate a lot of shit. At the edge of the room, a rudimentary bar had been set up and a man stood behind it, drying glasses with a dirty handkerchief and topping up small bowls with snacks. His involvement in this bit would be limited, but he was there nonetheless.

"Finally," said the man who they didn't know, and he clapped his hands together, joyfully. "I don't usually like cops, but you two..." He pointed at Murtow and Ricks. "Hang on a minute. I can't do... you're not standing in the correct order. Do you mind switching?"

Murtow and Ricks looked at each other.

They switched places.

Ricks and Murtow looked at each other.

"That's much better!" said the man in charge. "Yes, you two have provided me with entertainment these past two days." He stood; his chair made a horrible noise. "And all because you couldn't keep your nose out of my clit."

Ricks spat. It was meant for the floor, but most of it went on Murtow's right foot. "We don't even know who the fuck you are," Ricks said. "We know who *that* is," he added, nodding in the direction of Xavier. "That's Percy. But you? Not even on our radar, mate." He had fallen back into his quasi-Australian accent, which happened from time to time when he wasn't looking. If he really concentrated on his next line he could get rid of it. "So, why not let us go, and we'll all throw another shrimp on the barby."

Damnit! he thought.

"My name," said the besuited boss of bosses, "is Mr. Brandt, and my clit is the reason you find yourself in this predicament."

"Well, Mr. Brandt," Murtow said, wiping spit off his right foot, "I hate to break it to you, but this clit of yours, it ain't gonna make it out of this port."

"It already has, Detective Murtow," said Brandt, settling down on the edge of the desk. "It's amazing how security turns a blind eye when you offer them EVERYTHING THEY EVER WANTED!"

"Alright," Ricks said, wincing. "No need to shout, ya prick." Vladisvar, who seemed to have adopted Ricks as his own, gave him an open-palm slap to the back of the head, and for a moment things went fuzzy for Ricks.

"Gentlemen... *detectives*... I'm afraid this little game of ours has come to an end," Brandt said, and now he produced a gun from somewhere beneath his jacket. "It's a shame, really. I was starting to enjoy myself."

Ricks worked desperately at the plastic zipties, but Terry had been telling the truth: these were really high-quality zipties.

"My friend here, Mr. Xavier—"

"*Percival*," Ricks said, mockingly. It was childish, but so what? Who cares? Not Ricks.

"My friend, Mr. Xavier," Brandt went on, "has one final game in store for you."

"It's not much of a game, Mr. Brandt, but it'll be fun nevertheless," Xavier said, stepping up beside his boss. He produced a gun from beneath his jacket—where were all these jacket guns coming from?—and what appeared to be a gold coin from his trouser pocket. "It's called, 'If I toss an Eagle, I get to shoot Murtow in the face, but if I toss a Lady Liberty, I get to put a bullet in Ricks.'"

"Don't think it'll catch on," Ricks said, and he spat once more.

"Will you stop spitting on my shoe!" Murtow said, wiping it off. To Xavier he said, "Ricks is right. That sounds terrible. Can't we just play *Operation* instead?"

"No we can't!" Brandt said. "We're playing this one, and whoever Xavier doesn't shoot, I do, so that's that."

Ricks still worked at his ziptie restraints; Murtow did shakings of his head and mutterings of, "I'm too old for this shit."

"Right!" said Xavier. "Let's get this over with."

He made a whole scene of tossing the gold coin into the air, but once it was up, it went over and over in ultra slow-motion, the way they often do. All eyes were on the coin, and the coin went *whoosh!* for some reason as it came back down onto the back of Xavier's fisted hand and he slapped his other hand on top of it. The whole thing took less than a second, and yet lasted almost as long as *Titanic* (1997).

Xavier removed his hand; Brandt had a good shufty at the result. They both seemed happy at what they saw.

"Looks like I get the old man!" said Brandt.

"And I the mulleted Australian!" Xavier said. "On your knees, fellas. Let's do this the proper way."

"Who's he calling Australian?" Ricks asked Murtow.

"Who's he calling old?" Murtow asked back.

They were manhandled once again by the heavies behind them, and quickly found themselves genuflecting. Ricks gnawed nervously upon the rock-hard gum he had been carrying since yesterday. Velda's love-gift which, barring a miracle, he was about to take to the grave with him.

Murtow made the sign of the cross with his head, which was the best he could do given his restrained situation.

"Been a pleasure working with you," Ricks quietly said.

"You too, Ricks," replied Murtow, closing first one eye and then the other.

"How touching," said Brandt, pressing the barrel of his gun to Murtow's head.

"Such a shame," Xavier said, and his barrel, too, was put into place. "Are we going on three, or are we just going to shoot?"

Brandt shrugged. "Doesn't make much difference, really, does it?"

"Not really," Xavier said. "But it's usually good for tension."

"Can't be bothered with all that malarkey. Just shoot when ready."

"So it's not all drawn out?"

"And giving them a chance to get out of it," Brandt said. "Yeah, exactly."

"Yippee-Ki-Yay!" a voice suddenly said, echoing around the room. And a man, wearing nothing but a dirty white vest and a pair of dark pants, emerged from the shadows of a stack of pallets off to the right, depending on which way you were looking at it. He had his hands behind his head as he came out, which was, everyone present thought, somewhat odd, as no one had asked him to surrender yet.

All guns turned on the newcomer (so it wasn't just feet that did it for him?) as he slowly shuffled into the arena on feet bloodily adorned with slivers of broken glass.

"McLeod!" Brandt said, for he was the only one present who knew the newcomer. "I thought you were dead!"

"Yeah, well, you know what thought did?" McLeod said. "Your boy, Endo, did a runner."

"Ah," said Brandt. "That is disappointing. I'll have to kill him, his entire family, their friends, and their friends' families. And also *their* friends, and families thereof."

"Who's this?" Xavier said. "It's a bit late in the day to be adding new characters."

"McLeod's a cop," Brandt said. "NYPD."

Ricks, Murtow, and McLeod all acknowledged each other with a grunt, the way that cops always do when you put more than two in a room.

"He's here to kill me," Brandt went on. "For stealing his wife, taking every penny they had, adopting his kids and selling them to traffickers, and then throwing his dog in the canal—"

"You did what!?" Xavier gasped. "No, man, that shit's out of order. Dogs are lovely!"

"I loved her so much," McLeod said, holding back tears.

"And now you're going to die, too," Brandt said, levelling his gun at McLeod. "I can hardly believe this is how it ends," he added. "I mean, the way it's all come together, finishing here on the docks at midnight, with Ricks and Murtow and now McLeod, and my clit being unloaded as we speak. Couldn't have written a better script. Award-worthy, I think."

"Yeah," McLeod said. "But I'll bet you didn't count on this!"

And then, he made sudden movements, as if reaching for something out of sight. He spun around and threw himself backwards and forwards, grabbing for something just beyond reach. He grunted, too, and said, "Fuck!" and, "Shit!" He looked like a man being attacked by a swarm of bees.

"That's the NYPD for you," Ricks said.

Murtow nodded.

Presently, McLeod ceased his silly spasming, settling, sweating, slowly and surely, and breathlessly said, "Oxford, the prick! Duct-taped it too far down," and he turned around to reveal the Glock 20 taped to his back.

Brandt laughed evilly. Xavier did the same. Vladisvar and Terry had a go at it, but it was harder than it looked, so they quickly stopped. The big Russian went across to remove the weapon from McLeod's back.

"Do it fast!" McLeod implored Vladisvar. "Rip it off like a band-aid, otherwise it'll hurt more. Fucking hell, I can't believe Oxford did... and I came in here all cocky, with the 'Yippee-Ki-Yay', with bits of glass in my feet, and all that jazz."

"Never mind," Brandt said. "I'll bet you were crawling through shafts and everything, weren't you?"

"And smashing through windows," McLeod said. He hissed as the gun was ripped from his body.

"Yeah, I saw that," Brandt said with a fake smile. "That's gonna cost me quite a bit to replace, that is. Though it makes defenestration a lot easier."

McLeod didn't know what that word meant, so he simply nodded.

Mac the part-time bartender watched silently from the sideline. He didn't mind how long this went on for; he was being paid double-time.

Vladisvar nudged McLeod in the direction of the others. Once there and on his knees, McLeod grunted at Ricks and Murtow again and they grunted back.

"Can we get this over with now?" Ricks said, for he had had enough. "My knees are starting to hurt."

Brandt, Xavier, Terry, and Vladisvar all pointed their guns at someone who didn't have one, and were about to pull their respective triggers when all hell broke loose.

*

The SUVs ploughed in through the metal roller shutters, sending bits of wall and steel debris flying into the building. The three detectives rolled aside. A bullet, fired instinctively and unintentionally from Xavier's gun, barely missed Ricks's mullet, which had parted like the Red Sea in an effort to avoid the projectile. Murtow rolled over McLeod's legs, and the two became entangled momentarily, and lay watching helplessly as giant vehicles smashed into everything stupid enough to be standing still. Xavier and Brandt—the two misters—went their separate ways just in time to miss an oncoming Mercedes. Terry and Vladisvar ran for cover behind Mac's bar. Mac was already crouched down beneath it, drinking a large whisky and silently screaming. At the edge of the building, one of the vehicles slammed into a cage of gas-bottles, and they erupted like fireworks and shot off like missiles in all directions. One of them slammed into Xavier's back, taking him on a fifty-metre tour of the building that he had neither paid for nor requested.

Ricks's ziptie restraints had melted off, and he arrived, somewhat fortuitously, on his feet next to a forklift truck. For a moment, he looked at the forklift as if it were a piece of chocolate, because everyone—no matter *who* they are—fancies a go on a forklift when the opportunity presents itself.

Another explosion snapped him out of it, and he turned just in time to see the makeshift bar, and those within its vicinity, get wiped from the face of the earth. Terry's head went up in the air and the rest of him slumped to one side. The bartender guy, who hadn't been given so much as one line of dialogue, was plastered up the wall. He looked like a Halloween scarecrow. The big Russian was nowhere to be seen.

McLeod was up on his feet now, digging Murtow out from under the fresh rubble. Ricks saw that Murtow was bleeding, but he didn't appear to be too badly hurt.

What the hell is going on?

Ricks had no idea, but was one step closer to finding out when the passenger door to one of the vehicles suddenly flew open, and out stepped—

"Velda!" Ricks cried. "What the—"

But Velda was far too busy shooting at bad guys to engage Ricks in conversation. Her target was Xavier, it seemed, who had picked himself up from his magic missile ride and was now limping for the door. One of Velda's bullets nicked him in the shoulder as he went, knocking him slightly off course, but he made it to the door and disappeared through it, out into the night.

Four bulletproof-vested agents, who had emerged from the crashed cars, ran out through the collapsed shutters, shooting and yelling stuff like, "Freeze!" and, "Put it down!" One of them cried out, "Incoming!" and then there was the sound of another explosion, barely audible over the myriad Wilhelm screams.

If Ricks had had no idea what was happening a moment ago, now he was completely flummoxed. Why was Velda here? Why was she wearing a black bomber with DEA written on the back of it? Why was he just standing in the open like a sitting duck asking himself silly questions?

He dove for cover, and began to army-crawl toward Murtow.

"Where's the NYPD fella gone?" Ricks asked, once he was close enough to be heard.

"Went after Brandt," Murtow said. "Hey, Ricks, get me out of these zipties, will you? They're playing havoc with my arthritis."

Ricks fumbled around in the rubble until he came across a piece of glass. He cut Murtow free, then said, "This glass smells like feet," before tossing it aside.

Bullets continued to fly as Ricks led Murtow toward one of the crashed SUVs. Velda Brugenheim, it seemed to

Ricks, was a crack-shot, and a dark-horse, and also a damn good liar. Plus, hot-as-fuck, Ricks thought. He hadn't felt this turned on since that time he stood next to a forklift truck.

"Why's your girl wearing a DEA jacket?" Murtow asked, wiping blood and sweat and drool and bits of Terry from his face.

"I'm guessing," said Ricks, "she works for the DEA." Which meant that, and this really pissed Ricks off, she was probably earning more money than him. And *he'd* taken care of the bill last night at the chicken shop. And she'd *let* him! He made a mental note to bring it up during their next date. It was best to get these things out of the way at the start of a relationship, before they went too far. She'd appreciate that, Ricks thought, naively.

"Hey, Murtow!" Velda shouted. "You okay?"

Murtow wasn't. He had a hurty-back, and it felt like his insides had been blended, but he gave her the thumbs-up anyway. "Yeah! I'm good!" To Ricks he said, "She knows my name, Ricks. She called me *Murtow*." And he looked pleased with himself.

Ricks wasn't having that. "Don't worry about me, sweetheart!" he said. "I'll be fine!"

She nodded. "Glad to hear it," she said as a bullet thumped into the open car door she now found herself behind. She waited a second, then fired two shots toward Vladisvar, who had somehow survived where Terry and the bartender had not, and was now taking cover behind a brick pillar, sticking his big, bearded head out every now and then.

Ricks scrambled across to where Velda was firing from. "Hey, honey," he said. "I know we haven't been seeing each other for that long—"

She continued to shoot as he talked.

"But just what in the flying fuckery is going on?"

"I'm DEA, Ricks," she said, still firing.

"Since this morning? I mean, you were an accountant yesterday."

"I've always been DEA," she said, reloading.

"How did you know we were here?" Ricks asked, because even he didn't know they would be here until they already were, by which time it was too late to be anywhere else.

"That gum," said Velda, "is a tracking device, Ricks. I've been following you since I spat it into your gob."

"Saucy minx," said Ricks, taking the gum out to give it a quick once-over, for he was genuinely impressed. "Don't suppose you've got a spare gun, have you, darling?" he said. "Only Xavier's getting away."

Velda reached into the crashed car and came out holding a Remington 870, a model manufactured by Remington Arms Company, LLC, that is widely used by the public for—

213

"Not now, Murtow," Ricks said, for his partner had crept up on them both. Ricks gave him a clip to the lughole and pocketed the shotgun ammo Velda handed to him.

"Does he do that a lot?" Velda asked. She patiently waited for Vladisvar's head to make another appearance before hitting him square between the eyes. He grunted something in Russian before he dropped to the floor in an untidy heap.

"Only when he's nervous," To Murtow he said, "Stay with Velda. She'll look after you," and with that he gave her a peck on the cheek and trotted off after Xavier.

Velda looked at Murtow.

Murtow looked at Velda.

"Is he always like this?" she asked.

Murtow shrugged. "I don't know," he said. "I've only known him an hour longer than you have."

18

Sirens sang in the distance now; overhead, NBCLA News Chopper Four observed the mayhem at a safe distance. On board, as always, Terry Moreno worked himself up into a frenzy, commentating on the events in a wholly inappropriate manner, whooping and hollering at every new explosion as if it were a home-run in a Dodgers game. He would later be fired—not for this, but for a particularly ruthless tweet about the sudden death of Clint Eastwood (who he didn't, according to the tweet, have in his *Dead Pool*, snarf-snarf)—but for now he was in his element.

"It looks as though the bald guy in the filthy white vest is going after the guy in the pristine suit! And I have to say, I know whose side I'm on, and it ain't Baldy McBaldhead!"

Down on the ground, unaware that he was being made a mockery of for the benefit of at least seven viewers, McLeod pursued Brandt through the maze of containers that had been arranged into some kind of Pacman level. In some areas, containers were stacked two- and three-high. McLeod just followed the smell of bad cigars and whisky.

"It ain't gonna change anything!" Brandt called out from wherever he was in the maze. "It won't bring them all running back to you!"

McLeod didn't *want* them all back. He wanted vengeance for his dead dog. His kids had been assholes anyway, and Molly, well, Molly Generic deserved whatever bad fortune came her way.

But that dog...

Wicksy...

"You're a dead man, Brandt!" McLeod called back. "You hear me? Dead!"

There was a brief moment where neither of them said anything, just continued to wander amongst the containers, neither knowing where they were going or which way to turn next. And then, Brandt said:

"Hang on a minute, McLeod. You don't even have a gun, do you?"

McLeod looked down at his empty hand. Then he searched the other one, just in case, only to discover that Brandt was right; he was presently weaponless.

"I've got a gun, and you're coming after me *without* one," Brandt said.

"This doesn't look like a fair fight," Terry Moreno solemnly said up in the chopper. "The bald one's fucked up big-time here."

"Ha!" laughed Brandt. "Why don't you just stay put," he said, "and I'll come find you?"

Shit!

McLeod silently cursed Oxford Branning for being such an idiot. That Glock was supposed to have put an end to all this, and would have had it not been for Ox's awful judgement about just how flexible the average human being could be. Needless to say, the pawnbroker was in McLeod's bad books now, and would, peradventure, find a nice hefty brick had been put through his store frontage come morning.

"Are you there, Jim?" Brandt's voice was closer now, maybe only two or three containers away, but in which direction, McLeod couldn't be certain. All the gunshots and fireworks going off were terribly distracting. The hovering helicopter didn't help much, either.

"I'm gonna geeeeeet you!" Brandt sang. "And I'm gonna shooo oooh oooht you."

Come on, McLeod, he told himself. *You're the creepy-crawly through-the-vents, amongst-the-elevator-gubbings, barefoot-and-loving-it, master-of-wisecrackery, Jack-of-all-trades, ho-ho-ho sonofabitch!*

And he stopped, glanced up and about the place, and saw exactly what he had hoped to see, and it wasn't just luck or a strategically-placed MacGuffin. That crane-hook was there when he got here.

Honestly.

Post-haste, without further ado, and also all of a sudden, McLeod ran for the hook, leapt for it, pulled it as hard as he could—which, it being extremely heavy, wasn't very hard—and threw it forwards.

"I can smeeeeee llll yooooo!" Brandt sang, appearing from behind the end a Maersk container. By the time he saw the hook it was too late.

The hook smashed into his head.

Some of it went in, which was gross and also gratuitous.

And Brandt's feet left the floor, his body twitching on the end of the hook like a fisherman's worm.

Dead, but too stupid to realise it yet.

McLeod watched the body swing back and forth in the semi-darkness for a moment. Then, as was his wont (and since he was contractually obliged) he said, "And you thought I'd let you off the hook."

It was a pity there was no one there to hear it.

*

Ricks had Xavier right where he wanted him. He had chased him into a dead-end, and the only way out now was past him. Sirens and flashing lights announced the arrival of the cavalry; Velda must have been keeping Mahone and the guys down at the precinct updated. Of course she was. Just because she was DEA didn't mean she'd go over the captain's head to get this bust. After all, they were all after the clit; it just took a woman to find it first.

Of *course* it did.

Three black-and-whites pulled up and the sirens went off. The flashing lights remained, if only for dramatic effect. A taco stand was erected, and yellow tape was wrapped around poles and gates and snoozing dock-workers.

Out of the leading squad car, Captain Mahone emerged, and he took to drawing something on the ground with a piece of chalk. It was an outline of a man. "Try to get him to land in there," he said to Ricks. "Twenty bucks says you can't."

Just then, Percival Xavier came limping back. He didn't look too pleased with what he found waiting for him. The gun in his hand was raised, but pointing at no one in particular. When he saw that he was completely surrounded, he straightened up, smiled a little, and said, "Well, fuck."

Ricks had to give the guy credit; even with a shoulder wound he wasn't going down without a fight.

"You're not gonna use that shotgun, are you?" Xavier asked, nodding at the Remington that was pointing right at his face.

"Be a shame not to," said Ricks, already visualising the damage it would do. The blood and brains and bits of skull exploding into the air like a confetti cannon. He felt something twitch in his jeans, and he had to quickly think of his dead grandmother to prevent it from getting worse. That didn't help, so he crossed his legs and hoped no one noticed.

"Don't thoot him, Rickth!" It was little Officer Bossi. And there was Kowalski, also, and a couple of the other guys and gals from the station. And there was Uncle Henry and Aunty Em, though Ricks didn't know what they were doing here.

Mahone looked at Ricks.

Ricks looked at Mahone.

Mahone gave him a nod.

Ricks smiled.

"That's right," Xavier said, dropping his gun and kicking it away. "Let's do this the ol-fashioned way."

Ricks tossed his shotgun toward Kowalski, who probably would have caught it had he been given fair warning. As it was, it clattered him in the jaw and he went down like a sack of spuds.

"I've been looking forward to this," said Xavier, and he did crackings of his knuckles and grindings of his Turkey teeth before adopting that most famous of stances, the bare-knuckle drunkard.

Ricks didn't hang about. He moved in close, throwing quick, short jabs, snapping Xavier's head back each time his fist connected. There was quite a crowd now, gathered to witness the ultimate bout: suicidal cop versus playboy druglord. The rabble cheered and hollered. Yoko Ono had turned up, expecting to see her son, Endo, in the grand finale, for no one had told her he'd absconded.

Xavier hit back with a few solid jabs of his own. It had started to rain, only because fights always look better in the rain. And the lights from the squad cars beautifully illuminated the fighters. A photographer was down on one knee, snapping and flashing away. Someone told him to stop flashing, so he buttoned up his raincoat and sighed disappointedly.

Ricks threw a kick into Xavier's stomach, and the baddie almost caught his leg, but lost it thanks to the slipperiness of the rain which now coated both of them.

"Get him, Rickth!" cried Bossi, who may or may not have been watching the fight, it was hard to tell.

"Yatsu no burokku o tatakinomese, bora otoko!" screeched Yoko, which roughly translated to, "Knock his fucking block off, mullet-man!" and the translator with Ms. Ono told everyone what she'd said verbatim, for she was exceptional at her job.

Xavier lunged for Ricks, head down, and smashed into Ricks's groin, which hadn't yet begun to behave itself, no matter how much he thought of Ann Coulter.

Forced back into one of the squad cars, Ricks rained fists down onto Xavier's back, and Xavier went, "Ooh!" and, "Ugh!" and, at least once, he went, "Mmm, matron!"

Having none of that, Ricks let go of Xavier and pushed him back, kicking at his shins and slapping at his face as he went. In Afghanistan, Ricks had learned a new form of martial art called Chuckrati, but since there were no rats within reach, it would have been pretty damn ineffective.

"Hey, Ricks!" Xavier said, connecting with a swinging right to the temple. "Why fight back? You've wanted to die for years!"

Spitting out blood, and almost losing the gum-cum-tracking-device Velda had given to him, he said, "Things have changed, ya prick. Got a fine new partner and a kick-ass woman to boot." He threw an elbow into Xavier's face, knocking the baddie back and off his feet. He splashed down into a puddle; Yoko Ono started to sing *Toyboat* for some reason. A nearby deaf fella counted his lucky stars.

Ricks quickly dropped onto Xavier, one knee either side of the baddie's hips, and began punching. Once. Twice. Thrice. Quarce...

Xavier's eyes rolled back into his head so that Ricks could only see the whites. He threw a few more punches, decided Xavier had had enough, and climbed off.

"I'm not gonna kill you!" he said, not sure if Xavier could even hear him. "You don't deserve it that easy."

He began to walk away.

As they so often do when they think the job is done and there was a sunset, somewhere, that needed walking into.

Xavier—*Mister* to those that worked for him, *Percival* to his dear old mother—rose behind him in ultra slow-motion, gun now in hand, which he started to raise, ready to fire upon Ricks, roaring in pain and anger as rain came down onto him in sheets and diluted the blood from his wounds until it was thin and pink.

"Ricks!" shouted Mahone. "Look out!"

Ricks turned just as gunshots rang out.

And that, as they say, was that.

*

Murtow and Velda fired at the same time They had arrived just in time to see Xavier get to his feet. A second later and they would have been too late.

Xavier staggered backwards as the bullets tore through his suit. He should have been looking where he was going, because someone—no one admitted to leaving it there, so it would always be a mystery—had dumped a trampoline there, and Xavier somersaulted back, a Wilhelm scream piercing the night. When he landed, it was on his neck, which snapped, crackled, and popped.

Many of the gathered crowd turned their heads away to avoid seeing it happen. One of them—Yoko Ono's translator—turned her head a little too quickly, and she too suffered a neck break.

Ricks couldn't believe it. Murtow and Velda had saved his life, although later he would find out it was just Velda, really, as Murtow's six-shooter hadn't been replenished.

"I'll be damned," Ricks said, shaking his mullet.

McLeod arrived on the scene, and Velda was about to shoot him when Murtow knocked her gun down. "He's okay," Murtow said. "He's NYPD."

This seemingly incensed Captain Mahone, who, with a face like thunder and a body like an overfilled trash-sack, said, "NYPD? What the fuck? You have no jurisdiction here."

McLeod lit a cigarette, squinted coolly, and said, "Blow me."

Velda rushed across to Ricks and pulled him into a tight embrace. "Sorry I lied to you," she said. "We've been after these guys for a long time. When we heard about the clit, they put me in charge. Said only a woman would be able to find it."

Ricks nodded. She was right.

All the male cops and dock workers nodded and muttered things like, "She's right, you know," and, "I still haven't seen it yet."

"Hey, Ricks," Murtow said. "Not bad for an old man, right?"

Ricks wasn't entirely sure how much of a role Murtow actually played in the successful denouement taking place all around them. What he did know was that he was going to miss the sonofabitch when he retired at the end of the month.

"Captain," Murtow said to his boss. "I've been thinking, I'm not too comfortable leaving Ricks on his own just yet. If there's still a place for me, I'd like to stay on."

Mahone smiled and they shook hands. "Wouldn't be the same without you," he said. "Detective Murtow."

Everyone cheered; it was cheesier than a teenager's foreskin... probably.

"For *fuck's* sake!" Ricks said, completely killing the moment. "I mean, *thanks*, Reg. Look forward to the sequel."

"You can spit that gum out now," Velda said to Ricks, "and give me a proper kiss."

Ricks did as he was told.

And nice it was, too.

19

They arrived at the Murtow residence in Ricks's recently-purchased 1970 Dodge Charger. Matte black it was, and a classic, but best of all it wasn't, nor had it ever been, on fire. Not yet, anyway. He'd only had it for ten minutes.

"Do I look okay?" Ricks asked Velda as they walked, arms interlinked, along the path leading to the house.

"You look fine," snorted Velda. Ricks put fingers into her dimples, for he couldn't help himself. "Don't be so nervous. You've known Murtow... how long?"

"Two days," Ricks said, holding up the same number of fingers. "About an hour longer than I've known you."

"There you go, then," she said, stroking his arm. He was wearing a suit now, but no tie. He had drawn the line there. You start walking around in a tie, that's when you really are too old for this shit. "Just be yourself and enjoy it."

Ricks nodded. Velda was right. There was nothing to worry about. Murtow was his partner, and Tish, from what he'd heard, was a fine woman and a great cook. The seven kids, well, he'd figure them out as he went along, but Murtow had told him they were also great, even the white one.

Velda knocked the door, straightened Ricks's mullet, and waited. After a moment of waiting in silence, she said, "I love you, Ricks." Her dimples were so deep, a moth went in and came back out well-travelled.

He grinned, teeth like a hygienist's model. "I love you back," he said, and he gave her a gentle tap on the backside, for he was hoping to get to fifth base tonight, which involved the front, the back, and one of her dimples. She didn't *know* about it yet; he was hoping to surprise her over dessert.

Murtow answered the door and implored them to *come on in, ignore the mess, take your shoes off, though, and don't make eye-contact with the dog, or physical contact with the chinchilla.*

Detective McLeod, NYPD, had stuck around, and was, according to Murtow, hiding in the attic until dinner was ready. "He's still wearing that vest, Ricks," Murtow said. "Tish wanted to put it in the washer, but he wasn't having it."

And so they ate, and talked, and the adults drank wine and the kids drank soda, and boy, if they didn't have fun once the *Operation* board-game made an appearance. McLeod grunted and mumbled his way through much of the evening, but he was clearly having as much fun as everyone else, and he was thrilled to bits when a game of hide-and-seek kicked off.

Ricks was a great detective, but he needn't have been to quickly realise—and he counted them several times, just to make sure—that Murtow actually had eleven kids.

"Nah, can't be," Murtow said when Ricks told him. "Really? Eleven?" He spent the next twenty minutes rounding them up, and once he was done, he scratched at his bald patch and said, "No wonder we never have any milk in the fridge.".

It was a truly wonderful night, and even when it was time to leave, Ricks couldn't stop smiling. For he had made something of a family in the Murtows, and even promised to keep in touch with McLeod, too, just in case a sequel *did* come up.

"Never say never," Ricks had told McLeod.

"Wasn't that a *Bond* film?" McLeod had asked, lighting his fifty-second smoke of the dinner-party. To hell with Murtow's eleven kids and their virgin lungs.

Ricks and Velda said their goodbyes and headed back to her place, where the painters had finally finished, packed up, and gone off to their next job, to a new junk drawer they could search through while the residents were busy at work.

"So," Ricks said, turning the key in the lock and pushing the door open. "What do you think about journeying with me all the way to fifth base?"

Velda smiled. "I think," she said, licking her lips and producing a wet fish and a Pikachu costume from behind the sofa, "we should go straight to sixth."

"To quote Detective Jim Mcleod," Ricks said, climbing into the bright yellow outfit and giving the fish a quick sniff. "Yippee-ki-yay!".

Yippee-ki-yay, indeed.

THE END